False Start

False Start

Sandra Diersch

James Lorimer & Company Ltd., Publishers
Toronto

Morgan Elementary School

James Lorimer & Company Ltd. acknowledges the support of the Ontario Arts Council. We acknowledge the support of the Government of Canada through the Book Publishing Industry Development Program (BPIDP) for our publishing activities. We acknowledge the support of the Canada Council for the Arts for our publishing program. We acknowledge the support of the Government of Ontario through the Ontario Media Development Corporation's Ontario Book Initiative.

Cover illustration: Greg Ruhl

National Library of Canada Cataloguing in Publication

Diersch, Sandra
    False start / Sandra Diersch.

(Sports stories; 78)
ISBN 1-55028-873-3 (bound).   ISBN 1-55028-872-5 (pbk.)

I. Title. II. Series: Sports stories (Toronto, Ont.); 78.

PS8557.I385F34 2005   jC813'.54   C2005-900229-8

James Lorimer & Company Ltd., Distributed in the United States by:
Publishers   Orca Book Publishers
35 Britain Street   P.O. Box 468
Toronto, Ontario   Custer, WA USA
M5A 1R7   98240-0468
www.lorimer.ca

Printed and bound in Canada.

Contents

1	Joining the Clippers	9
2	Friends and Family	15
3	First Meet	20
4	Grandpa's Fall	28
5	Visiting	34
6	More Headaches	42
7	False Start	47
8	Left in the Dark	51
9	Surprise Visit	56
10	Back in the Pool	62
11	Bad News	68
12	Silver Valley	73
13	Focus	80
14	Grandpa Gives Up	86
15	Falling Apart	91
16	One Step at a Time	96

For Joan

Special thanks to Ellen and Shelley,
as always, for their advice and support.
And to Chris and Jenna,
with all my love.

1

Joining the Clippers

B ut I want to go back to soccer!" Caitlynn cried, kicking the table leg in protest.

"Caitlynn," her mother said, a hint of impatience in her voice, "we've been over this. Your ankle isn't strong enough yet for you to play soccer. You're going to have to choose something else to do this fall."

Caitlynn crossed her arms and glared at her mother, mutiny in her eyes. Mrs. Sinclair ignored her and continued looking through the pile of brochures spread across the kitchen table.

"What about ping-pong?" Caitlynn's older brother suggested with a grin.

"Shut up, Colin!"

"That's enough, you two," their mother warned. "Colin, where's the information on that ball hockey league? That looked interesting."

Her mom and Colin read the brochure together while Caitlynn continued to pout. She picked at a nick in the table and kicked her chair leg. Every once in a while she glared at her mother. She'd been playing soccer since she was five. It could be a bit nasty playing outside through the winter, especially when it rained, but otherwise she loved it. And she was lucky because she got to play soccer almost all year, since it never really got too cold and snowy to play in the winter.

It wasn't fair. If that dumb old Angela hadn't crashed into her, Caitlynn wouldn't have broken her ankle last winter. All those weeks in a cast had *not* been fun for any of the Sinclairs. Caitlynn scowled harder. If she couldn't play soccer, she wouldn't do anything! She'd refuse!

"That's an unpleasant face."

Caitlynn kicked the chair again as Grandpa joined the others at the table. He picked up a brochure about gymnastics and looked at it.

"I'm *not* doing stupid gymnastics," Caitlynn announced.

"Okay," Grandpa said and put the piece of paper down. "What *are* you going to do, then?"

"I want to play soccer, but Mom says I can't."

"Your ankle is still weak, Caty-Bear," Grandpa said. "It wouldn't be very much fun to be in a cast again, would it?"

"There's always ping-pong," Colin reminded her.

Grandpa put out his hand to keep Caitlynn from pouncing on her brother. "You know," he said, once Caitlynn had slumped back in her chair. "I have always loved swimming. It's a wonderful sport and very easy on weak ankles."

Mom looked up from the brochure and nodded, an eager smile on her face. "There was a brochure in here somewhere for the Maple Ridge Clippers," she said, and rifled through the piles of papers until she found it.

"I already know how to swim," Caitlynn said, but she sat up and took the pamphlet her mother held out to her. On the front was a picture of kids in caps and swimsuits splashing around in a pool. They looked like they were having fun.

"But you could learn how to swim better, faster. And there are meets to compete in," Grandpa said.

Caitlynn looked at him, her eyebrows raised. She'd taken a

few lessons and been swimming lots of times at Whonnock Lake in the summer. It was only a half-hour drive from Maple Ridge, a suburb of Vancouver. She always enjoyed being in the water. And she wouldn't admit it, but she was a little curious about that butterfly stroke.

"Swimming is excellent exercise, isn't it, Connie?" Grandpa said to Mom, stroking his chin as he always did when he was thinking. "I remember swimming in a meet in Kelowna when I was a boy. I was ten, I think — or was I eleven? Anyway, it was the first time I'd gone away from home for a whole weekend without my parents. I was nervous, but it was a great weekend. I think I even won a few ribbons!"

"You used to show me your album when I was a girl, Dad," Mom said, standing. She gathered the brochures into a neat pile and wrapped an elastic band around them. The ones for ball hockey and swimming still lay on the table. "You still win ribbons in your meets with the seniors team. Caitlynn, remember when Grandpa won first place last year for backstroke?"

Caitlynn started to giggle. Grandpa and her mom looked at her in surprise. "What's so funny?" her mom asked.

"I'm not dumb, you know," Caitlynn told them. "I know what you're doing."

Her mother and grandfather looked at her innocently, her mother even batting her eyelashes a few times. Caitlynn giggled again, and then she got serious.

"I really can't go to soccer?" she asked one last time. Mom shook her head.

"Then I'll try this swimming. But you have to take me to the practices," she said to Grandpa, "and stay. And as soon as my ankle is strong enough I'm going back to soccer."

"That's fine, Caty," Grandpa said with a smile. "I'd be happy to take you to your practices."

"Well, okay then. When does it start?"

* * *

By the first swim practice, Caitlynn was ready to forget about
the whole thing. Colin teased her for days, calling her Fish and
Flipper Girl, and making little fish mouths with his lips.

Then that first day she discovered she wasn't dressed right.
Most of the other kids at the pool had fancy blue bathing caps
and goggles. The girls had special swimsuits, all the same shade
of blue, with fancy straps and a white stripe along the side.
Caitlynn didn't have a bathing cap and she was using a pair of
Grandpa's old goggles. Her swimsuit was last summer's two-
piece with big pink flowers on it. She had loved wearing that
swimsuit on the beach all summer, but next to the beautiful blue
racing suits it looked silly and babyish.

She looked enviously at the other girls and sighed. Would
her mother buy her a new suit or would it be an "unnecessary
expense?" Since her father and mother had separated just over
a year ago, there had been lots of discussions about "unnecessary expenses."

Caitlynn tried to forget about her swimsuit and joined the other
kids as they got in the pool. She took a running jump and cannon-
balled in, holding her nose as she went under with a splash. When
she came up, Jim, the Clippers' coach, called her over to the edge.

"Caitlynn, from now on, please be more careful getting in.
You could have landed on someone jumping in like that."

Nearby someone snickered and Caitlynn spun around, but all
the faces were blank. She scowled at them and they moved away.

"Don't worry about them," a boy said. His spiky, black hair
glistened with water. He wasn't wearing a team swimsuit either.
"My name is Aiden Hamada."

"I don't like being laughed at," Caitlynn told him.

"Yeah, me neither. What's your name?" Aiden asked.

"Caitlynn Sinclair. Is this team any good?"

"I don't know. I'm new like you."

"They look pretty fast, don't they?"

"Oh well, you don't have to beat them or anything," Aiden said easily. "Just do your best, that's what my mom told me."

Caitlynn looked doubtful. She scanned the bleachers for Grandpa and he smiled at her and waved. She waved back, the butterflies in her stomach bouncing around like crazy. Maybe this hadn't been such a good idea after all.

"All right! Let's get this practice underway," Jim said, reappearing with a clipboard. "We're going to start with a bit of a warm up. I want everyone doing front crawl — six lengths, with a rest at this end."

Caitlynn swam her best, attacking the water as hard as she could with her arms and legs. When she needed a breath, she dog-paddled for a couple of seconds and then attacked again. By the time she got to the other end of the pool, she was huffing pretty hard.

She pushed away from the wall and kept swimming as hard as she could, even though her lungs burned and her heart was pounding. Caitlynn collapsed against the wall, embarrassed and exhausted. All the other kids were almost finished their second set of two lengths but Caitlynn knew she couldn't go any more. She could hardly breathe.

Someone kneeled down by her head. "That was a good effort, Caitlynn," Jim told her. "But you're going to wear yourself out before we even get started. I'm going to move you, Amanda, and Aiden into this other lane. Then you won't have to work so hard to keep up."

Caitlynn was very glad when that first long hour was over.

Finally she could have a shower and go home. Walking along beside Grandpa in the late September afternoon was the best part of the day. He even carried her bag for her.

"You did very well today, Caty."

"Yeah, right! I had to change to a baby lane, I was doing the stupid stroke all wrong, the other kids laughed at me, I wasn't wearing the right stuff, and I have to go back on Wednesday!"

Grandpa smiled and stroked her hair. "First days are always hard. We'll have to see about getting you some new goggles and maybe a bathing cap for Wednesday. But I don't think it was all bad, was it?"

"Well, Aiden's kind of cool," she admitted. "And I really liked that butterfly."

"It's a beautiful stroke, isn't it? When I was a younger man I enjoyed swimming that one."

"Well, Jim says I have to learn front crawl and backstroke properly first. Those big kids do it all so good!" Caitlynn said with an envious sigh.

"I always find it helpful to break things down into small bits," Grandpa said, adjusting Caitlynn's bag on his shoulder. "Just focus on one small part of a stroke and get good at that, then go on to the next thing."

"I don't know," Caitlynn said slowly. "There's all that breathing stuff and water goes up my nose when I swim on my back and I'm afraid I'll hit the wall. I don't think I'll ever get it right. And I'll never get to learn butterfly!"

Grandpa laughed and hugged her. "You are so impatient, little Caty-Bear," he said. "You want to do everything perfectly the first time! But that's not the way it works. Those kids have worked hard to swim as well as they do. They learned bit by bit. And you will too."

2

Friends and Family

"Caitlynn, do you know the answer?" Mrs. Singh asked at school the next morning. Caitlynn frowned and looked at the board. She did not like math. All the other kids in her Grade 4 class seemed to get all the numbers and fractions stuff, but Caitlynn didn't.

"Two thirds?" she guessed.

"No. Anyone else want to try?" the teacher asked, and moved away. Hands shot up all around the class.

Caitlynn sat back in her seat and drummed her pencil on the edge of her desk. Only ten minutes to recess. She was anxious to get outside with her friend Jenna.

Finally the bell rang and Caitlynn bolted from her desk. She grabbed a snack from her lunch bag and the bucket of sidewalk chalk she'd brought that morning from home. Then she had to wait for Jenna to talk to the teacher. She tapped her foot impatiently; recess was only fifteen minutes long — not very long at all, really.

It wasn't like Caitlynn's old school. There they'd had twenty minutes for recess and forty-five for lunch. And everyone there ate lunch in a big room, but here everyone ate in their own classrooms while supervisors walked around with clipboards and frowns.

Still, there were some good things about this new school. First, her brother didn't go to it — he was in Grade 8 at the high school. And the librarian didn't mind how many books you took out as long as you brought them all back on time. And they had three classes of gym a week, and right now Caitlynn's class was doing badminton.

"Okay, we can go," Jenna announced. She tucked a strand of dark hair behind her ear. "Did you bring the chalk? Good! I got a whole pile of stuff, look!" Jenna opened the grocery bag she was carrying so Caitlynn could look inside.

"Aw, cool! Where'd you find that?"

"My sister's makeup drawer," Jenna said with a giggle. "But don't tell her! She'd kill me."

Jenna was definitely another good thing about this new school. Caitlynn had been miserable when she'd joined the same Grade 3 class as Jenna last November. Her parents had separated and her dad had just moved to Alberta. Caitlynn, Colin, and their mother had moved from their old house in Coquitlam to the new one in Maple Ridge. Everything in Caitlynn's world was topsy-turvy. She missed her dad, her mom cried a lot, and Colin was always yelling at her. Her old school friends were busy, and she only saw her soccer friends when she had practice or a game.

But then Grandpa had moved into the basement suite in their house, and Jenna had become her friend. They liked the same TV shows and books, they both had older siblings, and Jenna's sister Tracey was a big pain, just like Colin. They both enjoyed making things up and had a great time creating stories about the people they knew.

Their favourite one was about Colin and Tracey. They'd been working on it since they'd learned that their brother and sister shared some classes. They didn't know whether the two even knew each other — not that it mattered. It was more fun if they didn't.

"So guess what Tracey did this morning?" Jenna asked as the two girls found some space on the pavement. "She put on her best jeans and shirt, and she spent an *hour* in the bathroom getting ready this morning."

Caitlynn found a piece of green chalk and began drawing. "Well, Colin put on *his* best clothes and he combed his hair. And he asked for extra lunch money, too."

"I think that they're serving meatloaf in the cafeteria today," Jenna said. "Tracey loves meatloaf."

"Colin was saying just last night how much he likes meatloaf, too!"

The two girls looked up at each other and suddenly began laughing hysterically.

* * *

Colin was already in front of the television playing a video game when Caitlynn got home that afternoon. She dropped her bag at the door and kicked off her shoes before joining him on the couch. He glanced at her briefly, then went back to his car crashes.

"What do you want, pest?" he asked, digging his hand into the bowl of popcorn in his lap during a pause in the game.

"Nothing. So how was lunch today?" Caitlynn asked, trying not to giggle.

"What are you talking about?" Colin glared at her through the dark shaggy bangs that hung across his eyes. "You're nuts."

"You know, you should consider cutting your hair," Caitlynn said. "I've heard that girls like to see their boyfriends' faces."

"Get lost, Brat!" Colin cried, swinging the joystick at her. "You are such a pain, Caitlynn."

"Has Grandpa gone to Silver Valley?" Caitlynn asked, giving up.

"I guess that's where he went," Colin muttered, focused on his game. He blew something up and coloured lights exploded over the TV screen. "Yeah! Take that!" he cried. Caitlynn made a face and went into the kitchen for something to eat.

At the dinner table that evening Caitlynn just picked at her tuna casserole. She rearranged the peas and carrots on her plate and tucked pieces of tuna underneath the noodles.

"You're not eating, Caty," Grandpa said.

"Not hungry."

"No wonder," Colin said with a smirk. "You ate about a dozen cereal bars after school."

"Caitlynn, we've talked about this," her mother said. "I have to be able to trust the two of you home by yourselves. Those snacks were supposed to last all week."

"I only ate two! Colin's a big fat liar!" Caitlynn cried. She kicked at her brother under the table.

"Hey, hey, that's enough," Grandpa said firmly. "Colin is it really necessary to tattle like that?"

"Aw, she asked for it. She was bugging me all afternoon."

"That doesn't excuse tattling."

"You always take Caty's side —"

"So how was Silver Valley this afternoon, Dad?" Mom cut in.

"It was busy. There were birthdays being celebrated. But Maggie and I had a good time. Right, girl?" Grandpa asked, smiling at the small sheltie sitting beside his chair. The dog's long, plumed tail swept the floor and she put a paw on Grandpa's leg. "I'm hoping maybe one of these times Caty will come with me."

"Me? Why do you want me to go?" Caitlynn asked, looking up from her plate.

"Well, I thought it might be a nice activity for the two of us. And if I'm ever not able to go, then you would be able to take over for me," Grandpa explained.

"Why wouldn't you be able to go?"

"If I got sick or something like that."

"I don't know," Caitlynn hedged. Visit with a lot of old people? Jenna said that whenever they visited her great-grandmother at her nursing home she was always confusing Jenna with her grandmother or a great-aunt or someone. Jenna said it smelled funny and Great Granny had a really small room. Caitlynn made a face.

"Caty!" her mother scolded.

"Never mind, Connie," Grandpa said, putting his knife and fork carefully side by side on his plate and wiping his mouth with his serviette. "It was just an idea."

3

First Meet

Caitlynn eyed the pile of funny-looking paddle things lying on the pool deck with suspicion. She didn't trust Jim. Last week he had made them all do some stupid thing called sprints. They'd had to dive in the water and swim as hard as they could to the other side of the pool, then climb out, walk around, and do it again. Caitlynn's lungs had burned and her face got hot. Now there were these thin, flat paddles with pieces of tubing attached to them.

"Do you know what those are for?" Caitlynn asked Aiden. Aiden shrugged as he picked one up and examined it. Then he tossed it back on the deck.

"Don't know. Ask Amanda." He grabbed a kickboard, pushed it down into the water, and sat on it, making a floating seat. Caitlynn laughed as he slid off and went under the water. He came up sputtering.

"What do we do with those paddle things?" Caitlynn asked the other girl in their lane.

"They're for your hands," Amanda explained. "You slip your hand through the rubber tubes and then swim."

"Is it hard?"

Amanda shrugged. "I guess, a little. It makes it harder to push the water. Jim says they help make your arms stronger."

Aiden tried to sit on the board again, this time hanging onto the edge of the pool until he got his balance. Then he paddled around the two girls.

"Were you in the Clippers last year?" Caitlynn asked.

"Part of it. I got sick in February and had to stop," Amanda said.

"Sick with what?"

"Mononucleosis. It made me real tired and I had a sore throat. I couldn't go to school, and I had to do work at home with a tutor."

Caitlynn looked at Amanda with respect. Imagine not going to school for months! She wondered how a person got that sickness. "I had tonsillitis once, but I only missed a few days. My brother Colin broke his leg really badly skiing when he was ten and had to stay home for a month because it was too hard to get him to school in the wheelchair."

"Wow," Amanda said.

"Okay, gang, here's the drill," Jim said, squatting on the deck. The crowd of nine- and ten-year-old girls and boys pushed in close to hear what he had to say over the noise of the pool.

Caitlynn listened carefully. She'd been caught not listening a couple of times and didn't want that to happen again. Mostly, however, she was doing pretty well. In the four weeks since she'd started swimming she'd learned how to breathe properly and do the backstroke. She was learning how to do the breaststroke. She liked being in the water, she liked the other kids — except Marcie who always thought she was better than everyone else — and she really liked the games they sometimes played at the end.

At the end of practice that day, Caitlynn felt pretty good. She had kept up with the others, and not made a fool of herself. She had even mastered those paddle things pretty quick. Then Jim wrecked it all by reminding them about the meet that weekend.

"For some of you it is your first time out. Don't worry. Just go and have fun. We'll practise starts and turns on Friday, have a bit of a pretend meet so you get the idea. Any questions? Caitlynn?"

"Is the pool going to be the same size as this one?" she asked. There were snickers from the other kids and Marcie snorted. Caitlynn glared at her but Jim quickly answered.

"Yes, the pool will be the same size. All the pools we swim in are the same size — twenty-five metres. Any other questions?"

There weren't any, so Jim let them go, reminding them to be at the meet by eight o'clock Saturday morning. Caitlynn climbed out of the pool and made her way through the crowd of kids to where Grandpa was waiting for her.

* * *

Saturday morning arrived far too early for Caitlynn's liking. Despite the mini-meet they'd had at practice Friday, Caitlynn didn't feel any better about what was ahead. What if she didn't hear the whistle and wasn't ready when the gun went off? What if she slipped off the big starting block and fell into the water like some dumb whale? What if she forgot how to do the strokes?

At least she had the same swimsuit as the other girls now, plus a new bathing cap and her own goggles. And Mom had bought a huge, blue towel and sewn Caitlynn's name in brightly coloured letters across it. None of the other girls had anything like that. Thinking of it made her feel more confident and eased some of the butterflies flapping around in her stomach.

Once the meet got started, things moved quickly. Caitlynn sat with Aiden and Amanda to watch the other kids racing. With all the announcements, the starter's gun going off, the splashing of the water as the kids swam, and the cheers of the crowd it was very exciting and noisy.

Jim came looking for Caitlynn and a couple of the other Clippers girls. He led them through the crowds of people and swimmers until they came to a big table. Behind it sat a man and a woman dressed in white. Caitlynn told them who she was and was handed a card. On it were her name, her age, the race she was going to swim, and the practice time she swam it in.

Jim patted her on the shoulder, wished her and the others good luck, and left them with another woman dressed in white who looked at their cards and showed them where to sit on the benches. Caitlynn's stomach did horrible flip-flops and she had to go to the bathroom badly.

She glanced up at the stands and found her family. Her mother waved encouragingly and Grandpa gave her the thumbs-up. Caitlynn waved back and then studied her card.

"What do we do with these?" she asked the girl sitting next to her.

"Give it to the people at the end of your lane and they'll hold it for you. When you finish swimming they'll write the time on it."

Caitlynn nodded. The people with the stopwatches at the end of the lanes were timers: Jim had explained that.

"Are you nervous?" she asked the other girl.

"Yeah. I've done this lots of times, but I still get nervous. Is this your first race?" the girl asked. Her swimsuit was green and white and had a shark across the front. Her bathing cap was green too, and had the word *SHARKS* printed on it.

"Yeah."

"Well, good luck," the girl said as the woman in white led their row out to the end of the pool.

Caitlynn stood by the timers, staring at the huge length of water before her. It looked so far! And there was too much noise and confusion. She wouldn't hear her family cheering. She didn't remember what to do!

The man who took her time card smiled at her as the whistle blew. "Go ahead, dear, climb on up," he said, nodding his head toward the massive diving block.

Caitlynn climbed gingerly onto the diving block. Were these ones bigger than the ones at her own pool? And was Jim sure the pool was the same length? The other wall looked awfully far away. How was she ever going to get there and back? She stared hard at the man with the starting gun.

"Swimmers take your mark!" he yelled. Caitlynn put one foot at the edge of the block and balanced the other carefully behind her. Her fingertips just touched the edge and she stared at where she wanted to land on the water, the way Jim had taught her.

When the gun went off Caitlynn's body seemed to fly off the block all by itself. The water was cold when she hit it, and her goggles immediately filled with water. Everything went blurry and the chlorine stung her eyes. Somehow, she made her arms and legs work the way they were supposed to. Somehow, she breathed when she needed to, and eventually she felt the wall. She turned around and headed back the way she'd come. And then, before she'd thought she had started, she touched the wall again and she was finished.

Caitlynn lifted her head out of the water and looked around. Just behind her, one other girl finished. She wasn't last! She wasn't first or second, or even third, but she wasn't last. She grinned. She'd done it!

The first time had been so exciting that Caitlynn couldn't wait for her next race. She sat beside Aiden on her fancy towel and cheered the others, but every time Jim came anywhere near her, she started to get up. Was it her turn yet? Her next race was longer — four lengths of the pool instead of two — but she could do it.

"Ready to go, Caitlynn?" Jim asked at last.

Caitlynn jumped up quickly. "Yup! But I can do it myself this time," she told her coach. "I don't need you to go with me."

"That's fine. Just remember that this is four lengths of the pool, not two."

"Yeah, I know. I have to go back to the shallow end. I'm not dumb, you know," Caitlynn told him.

"Well, if you're sure. Remember not to swim as hard as you can right at the start," Jim said. "You don't want to get worn out too soon."

"I know, I know!" Caitlynn said, waving him away.

She went up to the marshalling table and collected her card from the woman. This time she stepped confidently onto the starting block when the whistle blew. She tightened her goggles around her head, hoping they wouldn't fill with water this time, and then she took her position, ready to go.

The first couple of lengths were just like the first race. She kept her head down, didn't flail her arms all over or kick too hard, and made it easily to the second turn. But in the first race she'd stopped then, tired and ready to finish. This time she had two more lengths to go. Feeling her energy fade, she took a deep breath and turned around to go back one more time.

Caitlynn's arms felt like lead weights at the ends of her shoulders, and it got harder and harder to draw a breath. She moved slower and slower, sure with every kick, every turn of her arms, that her heart was going to explode.

She couldn't get enough air as she turned her head to take breaths so she dog-paddled for a few seconds. The end of the pool was miles away! Would she make it that far? She stuck her head down again, but there didn't seem to be any strength left in her body. A few seconds later and she was dog-paddling again.

Could she rest for a few seconds when she got to the wall? Would she make it back to the timers and her towel? Caitlynn was sure the pool was somehow a lot longer for this race. Finally she reached out and grabbed the deck edge, closing her eyes for a second. Suddenly she felt strong hands grabbing her wrists and then she felt the rough surface of the pool deck beneath her feet. There was Jim, looking at her with concerned eyes, his hand on her shoulder.

"Are you okay?" he asked.

"Yes. Did I finish the race?" Caitlynn asked, bewildered.

"It didn't look like you were going to be able to finish the race," Jim told her. "So I pulled you out of the water. I didn't want you to drown."

"What? I want to finish! They'll all laugh at me!"

"No, they won't laugh. You come sit down and rest. You're finished for the day."

Caitlynn stopped walking and wrenched away from Jim's hand. "What do you mean, *finished?* I have backstroke still."

"I'm sorry, but when you don't finish one race, you're disqualified from any others. I should have known that four lengths would be too much for you at your first meet. It was my fault and I'm sorry."

Caitlynn returned to her towel, ignoring the sympathetic smile Aiden gave her. She didn't want him feeling sorry for her. Especially since he'd not only finished his four lengths, but had come in fourth!

"Maybe you should try the kiddie pool next time, Caitlynn," Marcie teased. "I hear it's not as long as this one."

Amanda and Aiden jumped on Marcie before Caitlynn could say anything.

"You be quiet!" Amanda told her. "You didn't even try four lengths last year. At least Caitlynn tried."

"Yeah!" Aiden added. "You're not that great, you know. You just think you are."

Marcie opened her mouth like a goldfish, but no sound came out. Finally she closed it and walked away.

"Thanks," Caitlynn muttered, embarrassed. "I could have finished the race, though." She glared at Jim's back. She would never, ever forgive him for pulling her out of the water like that.

"Hey, Caitlynn," her mother said, crouching beside her. "How are you doing?"

"He pulled me out of the water. Like I was some kind of baby or something! I could have finished that race — I was just a little tired."

"No, sweetie, you weren't a little tired. You were exhausted and Jim did the right thing. I would have pulled you out myself in another second. Listen, you're done now, and you're cold. Let's go get you a warm shower and into some clothes. We'll go have a celebratory lunch, okay?" She started gathering Caitlynn's things together and putting them in her bag.

"I could have finished the race," Caitlynn repeated. "It's not fair."

"I know that's what you think," her mother said. "But Jim had to make a decision. That's his job as your coach. He thought you were in trouble and he did the right thing by pulling you out. There's always next time. It's not the end of the world."

It felt like the end of the world to Caitlynn. Marcie would never let her forget it and, despite Amanda and Aiden standing up for her, she knew they felt sorry for her. It just wasn't fair. She followed her mother miserably, not even cheered by the thought of lunch out.

4

Grandpa's Fall

Monday morning dawned clear and bright. Caitlynn climbed out of bed and looked out her window, a smile already on her face. She got dressed quickly and went downstairs. Her mother was sitting at the table with a cup of tea and the newspaper spread out in front of her. She looked up and smiled when Caitlynn came in.

"Good morning, Sweetie," she said.

"Good morning. Can I have Choco-Nuts for breakfast this morning?" Caitlynn got herself a cereal bowl and rummaged through the drawer for a spoon.

"I suppose. Not too much, though. Have you got your things ready for school?"

"Yeah." Caitlynn crunched happily on her cereal for a few minutes, reading the comics as she ate. She glanced up and smiled when her grandfather came up from his basement suite, already dressed and whistling. He kissed his daughter good morning and patted Caitlynn's shoulder as he passed. He sat in the chair beside her and reached for the paper.

"I'm going to do a shift at the bank this afternoon, so I won't be home when you get here," Mom said as she got up and put her dishes in the dishwasher.

"I'm okay by myself," Caitlynn said, milk dripping from

her mouth. Her grandfather stood up. "I'll even set the ...
GRANDPA!"

Grandpa pitched forward, his hands reaching out. He
grabbed at a chair but missed and fell to the floor. The chair just
missed his head as it crashed down beside him.

"Dad!" Mom cried, rushing to his side. She helped him up
off the floor and into a chair. "Are you all right? Did you hit
your head? Caitlynn, get Grandpa some water, please."

Grandpa's face was pasty white, and it took several seconds
before he managed to answer. Caitlynn stood beside him, holding the glass of water unsteadily.

"I just got up too suddenly, I guess," Grandpa said finally.
"I got a little dizzy."

"That's the second time this week that's happened, Dad,"
his daughter said, a tremor in her voice. "Maybe we should see
Dr. Assam."

"Goodness, Connie, don't be so quick to rush to a doctor. It
was just a little dizzy spell. I'm feeling perfectly fine now. See,
steady hands," he said, holding out his hands.

Caitlynn glanced at her mother and then back at Grandpa.
His hands were definitely not steady.

"You stay here and I'll get you some coffee, Dad. And I
think we should make an appointment to see Dr. Assam, regard-
less. It's been a while since you had an exam."

Grandpa waved his hands at her and smiled at Caitlynn.
"I'm right as rain. Honest. Now, I'm going to finish my coffee,
and then I'm going to take Maggie for her walk."

No one said anything as Grandpa calmly drank his coffee
and Caitlynn finished her cereal. Caitlynn's mother moved from
the counter to the table, hovering anxiously.

"Is Grandpa okay?" Caitlynn asked her mom a few minutes
later, as Grandpa and Maggie headed out the front door.

"I hope so, Caitlynn," her mother said, her voice tight and small. Caitlynn got up reluctantly, her eyes still on her mother. She was still looking out the window after Grandpa.

* * *

That morning Caitlynn missed several easy answers on a math quiz, and Mrs. Singh said her name three times before she realized she was being called upon. At recess Jenna found her sitting quietly on a swing. "Something wrong, Caty?" she asked.

Caitlynn sighed. "I messed up at the swim meet and Grandpa fell this morning. He *says* he just got up too fast, but I don't know …"

"Maybe he should go to the doctor."

"I think so. He doesn't want to."

"I'm sure he'll be okay. Don't worry," Jenna said gently, patting Caitlynn's shoulder. "But how'd you mess up at the meet?" She took a bite of her granola bar, then offered it to Caitlynn, who shook her head.

"Jim had to pull me out of the water during a race. He acted like I was going to drown, but I was just a bit tired!" Caitlynn dug her heel into the ground beneath the swing. "It was embarrassing! I know all the kids are going to make fun of me today."

"Aw, Caty, everyone messes up! I fell off Spirit once and landed right on my head. No one made fun of me."

"You fell off your horse?" Caitlynn grinned at Jenna. "That's a *little* funny. Did you hurt yourself?"

"Naw. Luckily I was wearing a helmet. Just felt dumb, like you," Jenna said, grinning back.

The bell rang. Caitlynn slid off the swing and followed her friend back inside. They had gym next, and she suspected that all those bad feelings were going to be even better fuel than a granola bar for running around the track.

* * *

That afternoon at swim practice, Jim had them practise their turns and starts. Caitlynn hated that diving block. The water looked so far away when she stood on it. She thought of the swim meet and the way her goggles kept filling with water. It didn't seem to matter how much she practised; she never managed to hold her head the right way. She looked enviously at the big kids who all dove in with no problem at all.

Aiden climbed up for his turn. He'd had his hair cut and the short little spikes stood straight up from his head, glistening with water. Caitlynn giggled.

"What?" he asked.

"Your head looks like a pin cushion," she told him.

"Be quiet, Caitlynn. I'm trying to concentrate." He turned around again and bent over, his fingers curled around the edge of the block.

Jim shouted, "Go!" and the swimmers all dove in. Some came up sputtering and coughing; others hit the water smoothly and swam a few strokes down the pool before turning around. Caitlynn climbed up for her turn.

"Swimmers, take your mark!" Jim called, and Caitlynn leaned over like Aiden had.

"Go!"

Caitlynn kept her head tucked like Jim had said, but then she couldn't see where she was going and panicked, raising her head at the last second. She smacked the water hard with her stomach and her goggles filled with water. She stood up, furious and sputtering, and tore her goggles from her face.

"That's okay, Caitlynn. Try again," Jim called. "You'll get it."

Caitlynn swam to the edge of the pool and climbed out. She looked up to Grandpa's usual spot. He was sitting with his back against the wall and was cupping his head in his hands.

"You okay, Grandpa?" Caitlynn called, moving toward him.

He slowly raised his head and nodded at her. "Yes, I'm just fine and dandy. That was a nice dive," he said.

"I landed on my stomach," Caitlynn told him, "and my goggles filled with water."

"Oh, well. Maybe next time you'll get it right. Have to keep trying, right?" he said. His face was pale and he blinked as though he was having trouble seeing properly.

"Did you get dizzy again?" she asked.

"A little, but I'm fine now, Caty-Bear. You go finish your lesson. Go on, now, Jim is waiting for you. I'm fine, honest."

Caitlynn returned to the pool to take another turn diving, but she kept glancing up at Grandpa. Most of the time he was watching, and he smiled and nodded to her, but then she'd look and he'd have his head in his hands again.

It was almost dark when she and Grandpa left the pool together a half hour later. Caitlynn tucked her hand in her grandfather's as they walked to the car. He looked okay now, but Caitlynn eyed him suspiciously.

She tossed her bag in the back seat and climbed in beside it. She buckled her seat belt and fished a cereal bar out of her pocket. She looked up, chewing happily, and found Grandpa holding his head again.

"Grandpa?" Caitlynn said in a frightened whisper.

He sat up and turned to smile at her in the dusky light of the car. "Yes?"

"Are you okay? Maybe we should walk home …"

Grandpa sat up. "Nonsense, Caty-Bear. We're not leaving the car in the parking lot," he said. He put the key in the ignition and the car hummed to life. "I'm just fine. The noise from the pool just gave me a headache, that's all."

"Maybe you should take something when we get home," Caitlynn suggested, watching carefully as Grandpa drove out of the parking lot.

"You're right. That's a good idea. And maybe I'll bring ear plugs to your practices — you kids are pretty loud."

Caitlynn frowned and leaned forward in her seat. Grandpa *said* he was okay but he wasn't acting like it. His knuckles were white on the steering wheel. He was sitting forward, frowning at the road before him, but they were hardly moving. Cars kept honking and passing them. Caitlynn was very glad when they finally pulled into the driveway.

5

Visiting

W ill you join me when I go to Silver Valley today, Caty?" Grandpa asked Tuesday morning, as Caitlynn was leaving for school.

Grandpa hadn't mentioned Silver Valley since the first time he'd asked her several weeks ago. Caitlynn started to make a face, but she suddenly stopped. It was only an hour. And if it was horrible, she could just wait for Grandpa outside.

"Okay, Grandpa, if you like," she said without a lot of enthusiasm.

"That's wonderful, Caty-Bear," Grandpa said, ignoring her tone. "Maggie and I will be waiting for you here at three." His smile was so wide Caitlynn was afraid his jaw would split. She nodded and finished tying her shoes.

Caitlynn had hardly made it down the front walk when the door slammed behind her and Colin came out, swinging his backpack over his shoulder. He pushed his uncombed hair out of his eyes and looked at her as he approached.

"What are you staring at?" he asked.

"Nothing. You need a haircut," she told him.

"Shut up."

Caitlynn stuck her tongue out at him. Was she going to be like that when she was thirteen? Because if that's what it was like, being all snarly and rude and sneaking around the house all the time, she'd rather stay nine.

"Did you notice Grandpa this morning?" she asked a few minutes later.

"Notice what?" her brother asked. "That he hogs all the newspaper? Or that he nags worse than Mom about cleaning up?"

"Did you notice how he kept hanging onto things when he was walking around?" she asked, ignoring his complaints. "You know, like the back of the chair and the counter and the wall and —"

"Yeah, so? He's an old man. He's not too steady on his feet. It's nothing."

Caitlynn kicked at a fir cone lying on the sidewalk. She hoped it was nothing. But he kept having those dizzy spells and he was still refusing to see Dr. Assam. "Well, he's not that old."

"He's not going to live forever, Caitlynn," Colin told her. "I know you don't want to hear it, but it's true. People get old and they get sick and they die. Grandma did. Grandpa will too, one day."

"Why don't you just shut up, Colin Sinclair!" Caitlynn cried, launching herself at her brother.

"Oh, get off! Geez, you always overreact to stuff! I said 'one day', not 'today.' Man, get a life!" He pushed her roughly from him and walked away.

* * *

Raised voices met Caitlynn when she let herself in the house that afternoon.

"But it's happened more than once, Dad," Caitlynn heard her mom say in the kitchen. "It could be something serious."

"It's nothing, Connie, nothing but an old man getting up too fast. Please stop hovering and fussing. It drives me crazy."

"I'll stop fussing if you would please just see the doctor. If it's nothing, he'll tell you so. But if there's something wrong, we should find out and fix it."

Caitlynn dropped her backpack to the floor and kicked off her shoes. The voices in the kitchen stopped. "I'm home!" she yelled and ran upstairs to change her clothes.

By the time she came back downstairs her grandfather was waiting by the door with Maggie prancing at his feet. The little Sheltie looked eagerly at Caitlynn and let out several excited barks.

"Maggie sure loves going to visit, doesn't she?" Caitlynn commented as they walked into the cool afternoon. It was nice to be outside in the fresh autumn air after the heat and anger of the house. Caitlynn hated it when Mom and Grandpa argued; it reminded her too much of the weeks before her father had moved out. She moved a little closer to her grandfather but concentrated on watching Maggie.

The little dog sniffed every leaf, every branch, every rock that lay in her path. Her tail floated behind her like a grand feather and her coat shone in the fading light. Grandpa always brushed Maggie before her visit. He walked her twice a day and fed her. Maggie was Grandpa's dog, although the whole family liked playing with her. If something happened to Grandpa, who would look after Maggie?

"Grandpa?" Caitlynn slipped a hand into his free one. It felt warm and safe. He looked down at her and smiled, but the smile was strained.

"Yes, Caty-Bear?"

"Why won't you go to the doctor?"

"Mostly because I'm a stubborn old man, I suppose," he teased, but then his face grew serious. "I shouldn't tease you,

I'm sorry. Your mother means well. She loves me and wants to take care of me, but to be honest, I just don't think a doctor is going to tell me much."

"Dr. Assam is real nice," Caitlynn told him. "He can even give needles without hurting."

"I'm sure he is a very good doctor. He takes good care of you and your brother and your mother. But I'm an old dog, and it's hard to teach us new tricks."

"You always tell me I should give things a try, even when I don't want to," Caitlynn told him. "Maybe Dr. Assam can fix whatever it is that's making you dizzy and giving you those headaches."

Grandpa laughed and squeezed Caitlynn's hand but he didn't answer. Caitlynn pulled her hand away and looked up at him expectantly, hands on her hips. But he wasn't looking at her; he was carefully watching the sidewalk ahead of him. After a while he cleared his throat.

"I'll think about it," he said. "Is that acceptable?"

"Yeah."

It wasn't long before Silver Valley appeared in front of them. Caitlynn reached for Grandpa's hand again as he pulled open the big glass door. Just inside, a wall of heat hit them and Caitlynn pulled on the zipper of her jacket. "It's so hot!" she whispered.

"You can take off your jacket," Grandpa whispered back.

Caitlynn stuck close to her grandfather's side as they made their way to the common room. Besides the heat, there was a smell Caitlynn couldn't name. It was kind of a mixture of cleaning stuff and old food. She wrinkled her nose.

The first person they met was a hunched man sitting by the door in his wheelchair. He leaned forward expectantly when Grandpa and Maggie came in the room.

"Hello, Old Joe," Grandpa said. He moved right up beside the man's wheelchair and Maggie sat down. "Maggie's come for her visit."

"What kind of dog is she?" Old Joe asked.

"She's a Sheltie," Grandpa told him.

"They don't let dogs in here. You sure she's allowed in here?" Old Joe asked. He stuck a hand in his pocket and rummaged around. "Don't have any treats. Sorry."

"Maggie is allowed in here, yes. We come every week."

"What's her name?" Old Joe asked, stroking the dog's silky head.

"Maggie."

Caitlynn looked at the man. What was his problem? Her grandfather answered patiently one more time. He told him what breed she was and how old she was, too. Caitlynn shook her head. Couldn't the old man remember anything?

Finally they said goodbye to Old Joe and moved on to visit with someone else. Mrs. Chen didn't speak as she sat in her chair. But she stroked Maggie over and over and smiled happily.

After Mrs. Chen they approached a silver-haired lady with a blanket across her lap. She stared straight ahead of her and played with the edge of the blanket.

"Would you like to visit with Maggie today, Elsa?" Grandpa asked.

"Don't know anyone named Maggie," the lady said.

"You've met Maggie before, Elsa," Grandpa explained gently. Once again Maggie sat down beside the chair and tilted her head up, nudging the woman's hand with her nose.

The old lady started to scream. Some of the other residents covered their ears and Mrs. Chen started to cry. Staff came running. One nurse led the woman away and the others calmed everyone else. Caitlynn looked desperately at Grandpa. He slipped an arm around her shoulders, holding her tight. When calm had been restored they continued with their visits.

"What's wrong with that lady in there?" Caitlynn whispered as they walked by the open door of the TV room. A woman sat by herself in her wheelchair. She leaned forward in the chair, held in place by a wide strap across her chest. Her body slumped slightly to the right, the arm useless in her lap, the right side of her face relaxed and sagging. Caitlynn shuddered and looked away.

"She's had a stroke, Caty-Bear," Grandpa told her gently. "She can't help the way she looks."

"What's a stroke? Why is she all saggy like that?"

"A stroke is kind of like when the lights go out in the house. That happens because the wires that run the electricity from the power station to the house get interrupted somehow. A stroke is when the wires in your brain get interrupted. It affects people in different ways. Some people might have a hard time talking properly, others may not be able to walk or use their arms."

"Can she think?" Caitlynn asked.

"Yes."

"I don't like it. Do we have to take Maggie to visit her?"

"As a matter of fact, Mrs. Dawson doesn't care for animals, so no. But if she did, we would stop to visit. It isn't very nice, I know, but remember that she can't help it, Caitlynn."

A half hour later they said goodbye to everyone and left. A blast of cold winter air hit them as they pushed through the doors. Caitlynn shivered and reached for her zipper. Grandpa turned at the corner to wave one last time, but Caitlynn kept walking, glad to be outside again despite the cold. What a horrible place — with all those old people, most in wheelchairs or leaning on walkers, staring at them, reaching for Maggie. They asked the same questions over and over and didn't seem to even listen to the answers.

"I'm sorry your first visit with us was so upsetting. It won't be like that every time," Grandpa said after they'd gone a short way.

"How can you stand it, Grandpa?" Caitlynn asked. "I'd hate to be locked up in a place like that. Don't those people want to get out?"

"I'm sure some of them would like to, yes. But they can't look after themselves anymore and there is no one else to care for them. That is something that happens when you get old, unfortunately. It could happen to me someday."

Caitlynn spun on her heel, her eyes wide her mouth open in protest. "No way! You won't be all drooley and tied to a chair. You'll remember Maggie's name!"

Grandpa smiled his slow, gentle smile and rested a hand on her hair. For several seconds he didn't answer her. He seemed to be thinking, to be looking far ahead of where they stood on the sidewalk.

"I hope I never have to leave the home I have with you, your brother, and your mom, Caty-Bear," he said finally. "But none of us can control how we get old. Some of us get old like my friend Mr. Arnott. You've met him — he doesn't look eighty-three, does he? But some of us are going to get old like Old Joe, who forgets things, or like Mrs. Dawson, who must be tied to her chair so she doesn't fall out. If I have to move away from you, I won't stop being your grandpa or loving you and your family very much. My insides won't change even if my outsides do. Do you understand?"

Caitlynn squirmed under his strong hand. It was scary to think of her Grandpa like one of those old people this afternoon, helpless and stuck.

"I don't think I want to go back to that place," she said. "I didn't like it."

"You know, it's nice for them to see a pretty young lady like yourself, with your happy smile. Some of those old folks don't have any family to come visit. And I like having you there with me. I like showing you off," Grandpa said with a smile.

Caitlynn walked silently for a while. She knew what he wanted her to do, but she resisted. It was so *awful* there. But Grandpa would be with her. The two voices fought in her head until finally she sighed. Some of the old folks had smiled and talked to her. One lady had even given Caitlynn a candy when Grandpa wasn't looking.

"I guess I could try another time," she said at last.

"That's fine, Caty, just fine."

6

More Headaches

Did you decide about the doctor's appointment?" Caitlynn asked Grandpa on their way to swimming Friday afternoon. Outside the car, rain streamed down the windows in rivulets.

"Yes, Caty, I did. I'm going to see him on Wednesday."

"Good. Hey, know what we're going to do in practice today?" she asked, brightening. Grandpa shook his head. "Relays. Jim says I can swim in a relay on the weekend. He entered me in one with Marcie, Meghan, and Amanda."

"I always enjoyed swimming relays. I swam anchor during a big meet in Prince George once. We came in first, too."

"Is anchor last?" Caitlynn asked. "Marcie says she always swims anchor. She says the fastest person goes last."

"Well, not necessarily. Every person on the relay is important."

"I told her that, but she doesn't listen. She always thinks she's better than everyone else because she's so fast. But this new girl, Meghan, she's way better than Marcie. I bet Jim makes her anchor this time. That will teach old Marcie a lesson!" Caitlynn grinned in anticipation of Marcie's downfall.

"That's not very sportsmanlike of you, Caty-Bear," Grandpa said. He looked over his shoulder, then carefully changed lanes before turning into the parking lot of the pool.

"You should all work as a team, not try to outdo one another."

"Well, Marcie's just mean. I don't like her. She's always calling me names like Creepy-Crawly Caitlynn and Slow Sinclair. She says I wasn't meant to swim, I was meant to sink."

Grandpa's lips tightened as he set the car in Park and turned off the engine. He shifted slightly in his seat and looked at Caitlynn. "Have you told Jim about this?" he asked.

Caitlynn shook her head. She was no tattle-tale. She could fight her own battles.

"Maybe I should have a chat with him, let him know how his swimmers treat each other."

"No! Grandpa don't, please. I can ignore her. I won't call her names back." Or go slow on purpose so Marcie had to go around her, then speed up. Or kick really hard right in her face. Or hide her towel, Caitlynn continued in her head. Grandpa studied her for several seconds.

"Let's get in, then, or you'll be late," he said finally and opened his door.

* * *

There weren't as many teams at the second swim meet, so there was room for the Clippers in the stands. Caitlynn, Amanda and Aiden staked out spots for themselves with their towels and bags before racing down to the pool deck for the warm up. Caitlynn thought about the races Jim had entered her in: 50-metre front crawl, 50-metre backstroke, and 50-metre breaststroke, plus the relay. No 100-metre races for Caitlynn Sinclair today! Caitlynn was kind of relieved. She didn't want to get pulled out of the water like a big baby again.

Mom and Grandpa were sitting in the bleachers near the team. Caitlynn smiled and waved and they both waved back.

Grandpa had had another dizzy spell that morning, and even now Caitlynn thought he looked tired. In addition to the butterflies in her stomach was a little ache of worry. Only a few more days and he would go to see the doctor, and Dr. Assam would fix him up good as new.

After their warm-up lengths, Caitlynn, Aiden, Meghan, and Amanda sat together playing cards, swatting each other with their towels and telling bad knock-knock jokes. When Jim called her, Caitlynn swam her first race and came in third.

After her second race, she ran up into the bleachers. Dripping water all over her mother's legs, she told them her time.

"That's way faster than last time!" Grandpa exclaimed. "You've been working hard."

"Well, I only came in fourth," she said. "That Marcie beat me again."

"Caty," her mother said with a laugh. "Marcie's been swimming much longer than you have."

"Yeah, well, she's been sick too."

Grandpa chuckled. "It's great that you beat your own time. That's the only thing that really matters …" He winced suddenly and bent over, his head in his hand.

"Dad!" Mom cried in alarm.

"Grandpa?" Caitlynn asked uncertainly.

"Just my head," Grandpa said. He straightened up and tried to smile. "It'll pass. But I think Jim is looking for you, Caty-Bear. You'd better join your team."

Reluctantly Caitlynn left her mother and grandfather and went to sit with her friends. She cheered them on in their races and tried to listen when they came back to tell her all about it, but her mind was on her grandfather. She kept glancing over, to check on him. Was he a little less pale? Was he sitting up a little straighter now?

At one point she went back to where he was sitting.

"Are you feeling better, Grandpa?"

"A little, Caitlynn."

"Can I get you something to drink?"

"No, thank you."

"Well, if you're sure," Caitlynn said, not moving.

"You go ahead and join your friends, Caitlynn," her mother told her, smiling encouragingly. "I'll take care of Grandpa for you. I promise."

Just before the starter began the breaststroke, Caitlynn looked up into the stands. Grandpa was bent over again, his daughter's arms around his shoulders. Suddenly the gun went off. Caitlynn slipped off the block and hit the water with a painful smack. She struggled to remember how to make her arms and legs work. Usually she enjoyed the breaststroke. She liked the sensation of the water sluicing over her head as she dove forward and the snap of her legs as she kicked. But today she couldn't get Grandpa's face out of her head.

At the end of the race, she didn't even wait to take her card from the timers. She raced up into the bleachers. Her mother wrapped her towel around her and gave her a hug.

"Caitlynn, sweetie," she said, her face worried and pale, "Grandpa's headache is really bad and the noise of the pool is making it worse. I'm going to have to take him home."

"I'm sorry, Caty-Bear," Grandpa whispered, his voice tight with the pain in his head, "but this is a bad one. I'll cheer from home."

"I'll come home with you," Caitlynn told them, moving to get her things.

"What about the others on the relay?" Mrs. Sinclair asked. "If you leave, they won't have four people. No, you stay. Mrs. Hamada has offered to take you home with Aiden. You swim really hard, okay? And we'll see you at home in a little while."

Caitlynn gave Grandpa a careful hug and kiss, hugged her mother, and watched them leave, her face creased with worry. She wished she could just go with them now. Grandpa didn't look great. His face was gray and, when she had kissed his cheek, it had been damp with sweat.

7

False Start

Caitlynn followed the other girls reluctantly when the relays were called. They'd practised all week. Each girl would swim two lengths of front crawl: Amanda would swim first, then Caitlynn, then Meghan, and Marcie would go last. Caitlynn had been looking forward to the relay all week but now the thrill had faded. She tried to listen to Jim's last-minute instructions, but her thoughts kept drifting away.

Was Grandpa okay? Had her mother found the pills that had helped before? Would this stupid race ever be over? It was hard to swallow around the lump in her throat, hard to focus past the tears swimming in her eyes.

The whistle blew and Amanda climbed onto the block. When the starter's pistol sounded, Amanda and five other girls dove into the water. Meghan and Marcie leaned out over the edge, screaming at Amanda to swim hard, but Caitlynn scanned the crowds again and again, hunting for her mom and Grandpa, knowing they weren't there.

She was startled when Marcie shoved her toward the starting block, pointing furiously at the water. Amanda was getting closer. Already? Caitlynn took a breath and let it out slowly, like Grandpa had shown her, and stepped up. The noise swelled and overwhelmed her. She couldn't hear her teammates, couldn't see her coach. Her throat ached, her heart ached, and her ears ached.

She saw Amanda beneath her and dove. Face down, Caitlynn swam as hard as she could. All she wanted was to get back to the wall and get out and go home.

At last she smacked the wall and felt the water rock around her as Meghan dove in. She climbed out of the pool and stood shivering on the deck while she waited for Meghan and then Marcie to swim their lengths.

Marcie was still in the water when a meet official came to talk to Jim. Caitlynn, Amanda, and Meghan stood at the edge of the pool yelling at Marcie, who was in first place. At the last second, the girl in the next lane passed her, but the Clippers team was second. The others pulled Marcie out of the pool, patting each other on the back, congratulating themselves.

"Girls," Jim said, breaking into their celebrations. They turned to look at him. "I'm sorry, but the team has been disqualified. There was a false start." Jim sighed and rubbed his hand across his forehead as the girls cried out in objection. "Caitlynn, you dove in before Amanda had touched the wall. I'm sorry, girls. It was a great race. You did very well ..."

"Caitlynn! I don't believe it! Why didn't you pay attention?" Amanda demanded angrily.

"I didn't do it on purpose!" Caitlynn cried.

"We were second! Geez, Caitlynn, you are so dumb!" Marcie yelled, throwing her hands in the air, her face flushed.

"I told you, I didn't do it on purpose!" Caitlynn screamed, tears running down her cheeks.

Jim stepped in quickly and separated them. He spoke quietly to Marcie and the others first, and then turned to Caitlynn. "I'm sorry your grandfather isn't feeling well. I know your mind is somewhere else. Don't worry about the others; they'll get over it. Now, you go get dressed. Mrs. Hamada will be waiting for you in the lobby." He gave her shoulder a quick squeeze and Caitlynn nodded.

* * *

Caitlynn sat forward in her seat, staring out the window, hoping to see her mother's car parked in the driveway. But as the station wagon approached the house, Caitlynn could see there was no car parked out front. Her heart pounded harder and a horrible dread filled her.

Caitlynn flew from the car before it had even come to a stop and crashed through the front door. She hurried through the rooms, searching frantically, not even noticing that Mrs. Hamada was following her into the house. Finally she found Colin sitting at the kitchen table with their mother's friend, Mrs. Farina, sitting beside him. Open books lay on the table in front of them.

"Where's Mom and Grandpa?" Caitlynn asked her brother. Colin opened his mouth to answer but closed it again as tears filled his eyes. He blinked hard and turned away to hide his face.

"Caitlynn, your grandfather had to go to the hospital," Mrs. Farina said gently, getting up and moving Caitlynn to a chair at the table. "He had a stroke just after they got home. I'm so sorry, dear. Your mother is with him at the hospital. I'm going to stay here with you and your brother until your mom can come home."

"Oh dear, how awful," Mrs. Hamada said softly.

She sat down beside Caitlynn and took her hand. Colin sniffed and the furnace clicked on. A car horn sounded from out on the road. Caitlynn looked from her brother to the two women, blinking. There was something wrong with her eyes and her ears. She shook her head. It was as though fog had rolled into the kitchen and settled in her head. She couldn't focus, couldn't hear anything but a rush and roar. She blinked and began to shake.

"Is he dead?" she whispered in a choked voice.

"No," Mrs. Farina said firmly. "Your mother phoned twenty minutes ago to say he was stable. That means that his heart and breathing are okay. He's not going to die."

Vaguely, over the roaring in her ears, Caitlynn heard Mrs. Hamada asking Mrs. Farina questions and Mrs. Farina answering. Colin shifted in his seat and wiped his arm across his face. Mrs. Farina reached over and rubbed his shoulder, but he pulled away from her touch. Caitlynn shook even harder. Colin was afraid! Colin, who was always complaining about Grandpa nagging, who was never afraid of anything! Aiden's mother wrapped her arms around Caitlynn's shivering shoulders and Caitlynn buried her head in Mrs. Hamada's chest.

They were still sitting together like that an hour later when Mom came through the door. Caitlynn broke away from Mrs. Hamada and threw herself into her mother's arms, finally letting the tears come.

8

Left in the Dark

I just don't think it's a good idea, Diane," Mom said. "It will be upsetting."

"What's upsetting the children," Mrs. Farina said, "is the not knowing. Every day Caitlynn is asking me question after question. She doesn't believe any of what I tell her. Seeing your dad in the hospital with the tubes and monitors will be scary, but at least they will know he's still alive. I know it isn't my business, Connie, but I think you should take them."

Her mother didn't know Caitlynn was crouched behind the doorway, listening to their conversation in the kitchen. If they found her, she'd catch heck, but it was worth the chance. She had to know what was going on.

"I think I'd like to wait a little longer," Caitlynn heard her mom say slowly. "I know it isn't easy — you're wonderful to watch them for me — but I just don't think it's the right time."

Caitlynn held her breath. She wanted to go so badly! She was sure her mother was keeping things from her, despite what Mrs. Farina told her. Upstairs Colin slammed a door and Caitlynn couldn't hear anything from the kitchen. When she could hear again, they'd changed the subject.

"You should have something to eat, Connie," Mrs. Farina said. "Did you have lunch?"

"Oh, I grabbed something in the cafeteria while Dad was napping. But I am hungry. I guess I should think about something for dinner."

Caitlynn heard the fridge door open with a little sucking noise. Her own stomach growled and she covered it with her hand, alarmed. When no angry parent came dashing from the kitchen, she let out her breath. She stood up and went in to the kitchen.

"Caitlynn! Where did you come from?" her mother asked, hugging her tight.

"I was in my room. Can I have something to drink?" she asked.

Mom poured her a glass of milk and Caitlynn sipped at it slowly. She hoped they'd talk some more about Grandpa but instead they discussed the week's schedule.

"And Caitlynn, you've missed two swim practices this week. I think Friday you need to go back. Mrs. Hamada said she'd be happy to take you."

"Do I have to?" Caitlynn asked.

"Well, yes, you should go back to practice."

"Grandpa always took me. I don't want to go if he can't take me."

"Grandpa would want you to keep going, Caitlynn," her mother said softly. "He wouldn't want you to give up. He's not giving up."

Caitlynn sniffed. On Tuesday Maggie had sat by the door for hours waiting to go to Silver Valley. Caitlynn couldn't drag the dog away from her waiting place until she put her leash on and took her for a walk.

Warm salty tears ran down Caitlynn's cheeks. At the tug of her mother's hand on hers, Caitlynn climbed into her mother's lap.

"Everything's all wrong without Grandpa here," she whispered against the soft cotton of her mom's shirt. It smelled of fruit and the warm, clean scent that was her mom.

She rubbed Caitlynn's back gently in circles, and Caitlynn heard a small sob deep in her mom's chest. "I know, I know. But he's working hard at getting better, Caitlynn. In the meantime, it helps Grandpa to know we are doing all the things we usually do …"

"Like going to the pool," Caitlynn finished with a sigh. "Well, okay, I'll go with Mrs. Hamada tomorrow."

"That's my girl," her mother said, squeezing her.

To be honest, Caitlynn had missed the water. At home there was nothing to do but miss Grandpa and stay out of Colin's way. He was always banging around the house, yelling at her or Maggie. It would be good to be with her friends.

Mrs. Farina stood up and took the empty cups and glasses to the counter.

"Please leave those things, Diane. You've done so much for us already," Caitlynn's mom said. She patted Caitlynn on the hip and they both stood up.

"You know I don't mind, Connie."

The two friends hugged each other for a long time before Mrs. Farina left. Mom pulled a casserole out of the fridge and slid it into the oven. She put the dishes into the dishwasher and then turned around, dishtowel in hand.

"I'm going to go upstairs and have a quick shower and change my clothes, Caitlynn," she said, drying her hands. "Will you set the table and feed Maggie, please? I'll get Colin to come down and make a salad. We'll eat in a half hour."

"I want to see Grandpa."

Her mother sighed. Slowly she folded the towel and slid it onto the rack. "I know you do, sweetie, but …"

"I want to see him! It's not fair!" Caitlynn stamped her foot.

"You said he's doing well. You said he still looks like Grandpa, so why can't I see him? He misses me! I know he does!"

"Oh, Caitlynn." Mom's voice filled with tears. "I know you miss him, and he does miss you very much. But …"

"You're mean! I hate you!" Caitlynn fled from the kitchen and threw herself on her bed, sobbing into her pillow.

* * *

Friday morning Caitlynn walked slowly along the sidewalk, dragging her backpack. She was tired and grouchy and frustrated. Another appeal to her mother at breakfast had failed. Caitlynn didn't know what to do. She missed Grandpa so much it hurt all the time. Couldn't her mom see that?

She was lost in her thoughts when Jenna bounced up beside her. "Morning!" she said cheerily. When Caitlynn grunted an answer, some of the spring went out of her friend and her shoulders slumped. "Want to hear what Tracey did last night? She —"

"Not really," Caitlynn interrupted.

"What's wrong, Caty?" Jenna asked, touching her elbow. "Did something happen to your Grandpa?"

"I wouldn't know, I'm not allowed to see him." She kicked a rock lying on the sidewalk and sent it flying onto the road.

"Still? Didn't you ask your mom?"

"Yeah, a couple of times. She keeps saying no."

"Did you tell her that I went to see my grandma when she broke her leg?" Caitlynn shook her head. "That's too bad, Caty. I know how much you miss him."

Her friend's sympathy made Caitlynn's eyes blurry with tears. She wiped at her face angrily. Jenna pulled an apple out of her backpack and took a bite.

"Want some?" she asked.

"No thanks ..." Caitlynn said, as a small thought crept into her head.

Jenna crunched on her apple, and Caitlynn kicked more rocks. Eventually the school appeared in front of them with the crowds of kids running and yelling over the playground and fields. Caitlynn stopped walking. Jenna threw her apple core in the garbage can and shifted her backpack.

"You want to come over to my house after school? Do you think your mom would let you? I got this really cool new jewelry-making kit. We could make —"

"No, I can't," Caitlynn interrupted. "I've got swimming."

Jenna's face fell and she shrugged. "Well, okay. Maybe next week."

"Yeah, maybe," Caitlynn agreed absently. She looked down the street, past the school, and her eyes narrowed.

"You coming? The bell's going to ring in a minute," Jenna said, glancing at her watch.

"You go ahead. I'll catch up with you," Caitlynn told her, deciding what she was going to do.

"Okay. Don't be late!" Jenna called as she ran off.

9

Surprise Visit

As soon as Jenna was out of sight, Caitlynn ran. She knew where the hospital was. If she hurried, she could get there and see for herself that Grandpa looked like Grandpa, that he was not a hunched-over, drooling mess, and then get back to school by recess.

The hospital, a low stone building nestled in trees and surrounded by parking lots, was only a few blocks from Caitlynn's school. It was a busy place, with cars and ambulances, doctors and nurses and visitors coming and going constantly. Caitlynn went through the large glass front doors, acting like she knew where she was going and had permission to be there.

The first thing she noticed was the smell — cleaner, food, and something she couldn't name. It was similar to the smell at Silver Valley, and she wrinkled her nose. Poor Grandpa! She would have to bring him something good to smell.

The elevator was waiting, and she was quickly whisked upstairs to the third floor. She managed to find Grandpa's room by following the signs posted on the walls, but hesitated at the door. Three of the four beds were occupied — which one was Grandpa's?

"Who are you looking for, little girl?" one of the men asked, motioning her forward.

Caitlynn stepped slowly into the room. It was warm and stuffy, and the windows faced another part of the hospital, letting in just a little light.

"I'm looking for my grandpa," she said softly.

"Well, what's his name?" the man asked, coughing a phlegmy, chest-rattling cough. He put a tissue to his mouth. Caitlynn hoped whatever he had wasn't contagious.

"Peter Wilson," she said.

"Well, sure, he's right there by the window. Kind of dozy this morning, but probably if you poke him, he'd wake up. He sleeps a lot."

Caitlynn walked slowly toward the bed by the window. The man in the hospital bed wearing the pale blue hospital gown looked nothing like Grandpa. His mouth hung open slightly as he slept and his chin touched his chest. His whole body leaned to the left. Every once in a while he twitched, like Maggie sometimes did as she dreamed. One side of his face drooped a bit and he needed a shave. This wasn't her Grandpa, was it?

But then Caitlynn saw the small, framed photograph of herself, her mother, and Colin. Grandpa had taken it last Christmas, and usually it sat by his bed at home. Tears filled Caitlynn's eyes. It was Grandpa.

For a second, Caitlynn couldn't decide what to do, where to go. What had they done to him? He'd been fine when he left the pool. Just a headache. And now! Now, he was just like Mrs. Dawson. Horrid Mrs. Dawson in the wheelchair! Caitlynn choked on her sobs and turned away.

"Caitlynn!" Her mother stood in the doorway holding a cup of something steamy.

"What have they done to Grandpa?" Caitlynn demanded. She wiped at her wet face with the back of her hand, and then smeared the snot and tears across her jeans.

"Oh, Caty, Caty. This was why I didn't want you to come! How did you get here? Why aren't you in school?" Her mother peppered her with questions as she crossed the room. She set her coffee down on the tall table by the bed and crouched in front of Caitlynn.

"I came because no one would tell me anything. I wanted to see! He looks just like Mrs. Dawson. Can they fix him? Can they make him better?"

Her mother put her arms around Caitlynn and held her tightly. "Why don't we go out in the hall and talk?" she suggested. "Then we won't disturb these other gentlemen."

"I'm sorry, Caitlynn," her mother began when they were sitting together on the hard chairs in the hallway. "I guess I was wrong to hide the truth from you. The thing is, Grandpa's stroke was, was ..." she paused, took a long, deep breath and let it out slowly. "His stroke was pretty bad. There is a lot of injury to his brain. Part of the brain that got hurt was the part that helps him control his face muscles and lets him talk. So Grandpa can't speak very well just now. Hopefully he'll be able to talk better with help from the therapist. He also lost some of the control of his left arm and leg, so he can't walk."

Caitlynn tried to shut off her mother's words. It was all a dream, a bad dream, and if she concentrated hard enough she would wake herself up. She put her hands to her ears but her mother pulled them gently away again.

"Caitlynn, please listen. You came here because you wanted the truth and that's what I'm giving you. It's going to take a lot of hard work, but Grandpa will gradually regain the use of his arm and leg and he will be able to talk to us. We have to work hard at helping him."

"When can he come home?" Caitlynn asked. "I'll do all that exercise stuff with him, if they show me how. I'll even stay home from school."

Mom smiled and brushed the unruly red hair back from Caitlynn's face. Her own face was damp with tears too, and her glasses were smeared. "That is a wonderful offer, but I think it would be best if we let the doctors and therapists do their jobs and we did ours, which is to love Grandpa and support him and help him get better by visiting him."

"When can he come home?"

"Not for a while, Caitlynn. But in the meantime, would you come back in the room with me and say hi? Then I'm taking you back to school."

Caitlynn waited in the lounge while her mother made a quick call to the school; then, hand in hand, they made their way back to Grandpa. His eyes were open as they came in the room, and he watched as Caitlynn and her mother approached the bed.

"Good morning, Dad," Mom said, taking her father's hand and kissing his bristly cheek. "I brought a visitor for you."

Caitlynn stood awkwardly at the side of the bed, kept at a distance by the metal railing. Green hospital blankets were pulled up over Grandpa's legs and chest, and she could see the outline of his legs beneath them. He looked thin and small, not tall and strong like the Grandpa who went visiting the old people at Silver Valley. This man looked old too.

"Why don't you tell Grandpa about Maggie," her mother suggested.

"She misses you, Grandpa," Caitlynn began awkwardly. It felt strange to speak normally to this stranger, as though it was just another chat by her grandfather's chair at home. "Colin and me take turns taking her for walks and we feed her. Maybe she can come and visit you!"

Garbled noise came out of her grandfather's mouth. Caitlynn spun around to stare at her mother, who smiled and nodded. "He said he'd like that."

Caitlynn turned back to Grandpa. "I'll brush her and put on her little scarf and she can sit up on the bed for you to pat her!"

Grandpa said something in reply, and Caitlynn looked to her mother to translate. "He said maybe you could visit some of the other patients, too."

"How do you know what he's saying?" Caitlynn asked. "It just sounds like nonsense to me, not like Grandpa at all."

"We've been talking together all week, and I listen very hard. I don't understand everything, but enough. And you will too, once you get used to it."

Caitlynn nodded, not entirely convinced. She turned back to the bed. "Sure, Grandpa, Maggie and I could say hi to the other people."

He nodded ever so slightly. "Goo gul," he said. "Goo Cay-Ba."

"You said my name!" Caitlynn cried. "You said Caty-Bear, I heard it! I heard it Mom!" She leaned over and hugged him, despite the IV drip and the bars. They sat together happily for a few seconds, enjoying the moment. Then Grandpa spoke again.

"'Ow shwim?" he asked. Caitlynn frowned at him. "'Ow shwim?" he said again more slowly. Caitlynn grinned, nodding.

"I'm going back to the pool today. Mrs. Hamada is going to take me."

"Ow eelay?"

"What?" Caitlynn asked.

"Ow eelay?" Grandpa said again, more slowly.

"I'm sorry Grandpa, I don't understand." She turned to her mother, but she just shook her head. Grandpa tried again, getting more and more agitated with each effort until finally his daughter moved closer to try to soothe him. He pulled away from her and hit the bed with a weak smack, shaking his head in frustration.

"Ow eeeelaaay," he tried one last time, and a little light went on in Caitlynn's head.

"How was the relay? That's what you're asking, right?"

Relief swept over Grandpa's tense face, and he nodded. Caitlynn grinned but then her face grew sober again.

"I dove in too soon, Grandpa," she confessed, her cheeks growing hot. "We got disqualified. Marcie's real mad at me."

"Ecks ime," Grandpa told her, patting her hand. Caitlynn frowned again, shaking her head.

After three more tries, Caitlynn got it.

"Yeah, next time," she agreed.

"Dad, I think it's time you rested, and Caitlynn needs to go to school," Caitlynn's mom said at last, standing.

Caitlynn gave Grandpa one last hug and kissed his cheek. "You need a shave," she whispered and giggled when he brushed his whiskers across her cheek. "I'll come back soon, 'kay?"

He nodded and squeezed her hand. Then Caitlynn followed her mom out of the room.

10

Back in the Pool

Part way through the afternoon, Caitlynn began to have second thoughts about going back to swim practice. The last time she'd seen her teammates, they'd all been very angry with her for that darn false start. What if they were still mad? What if they didn't want her to come back? The more she thought about it, the less she wanted to go. By the time she got home she was a mess.

"Get out of the way, you stupid dog!"

Maggie tucked her tail between her legs and scurried to her basket. Caitlynn flung her backpack on the floor and kicked off her shoes. Her stomach was in knots and her shoulders felt tight and sore.

Her mother came out of the kitchen, a basket of freshly folded clothes under her arm. "Hi, Sweetie. How was your day? Mrs. Hamada just called. She'll be here in twenty minutes," she said.

"Call her back and tell her not to bother. I'm not going."

Mom stopped, one foot resting on the bottom stair. She frowned at Caitlynn. "What do you mean you're not going?"

"Just what I said. I'm not going!" Caitlynn threw her coat in the closet and slammed the door shut. It swung open again and hit her. "CLOSE!" she cried, slamming it again.

Her mother put the basket down and came over to Caitlynn. She closed the closet door and, taking Caitlynn by the shoulders, walked them both to the couch. "Why don't you tell me what happened today that's made you so upset."

"I'm not going to the pool," Caitlynn said again, sitting rigidly beside her mom. "They don't want me there. They're all mad at me!"

"Who's they?"

"Marcie and Amanda and Meghan. They're all mad at me for getting our relay disqualified. I know they're glad I didn't come back!" Caitlynn wiped at her damp eyes.

"Did someone tell you they were still angry?" her mother asked, rubbing Caitlynn's back with the palm of her hand.

"No."

"Well, how do you know they're still angry? I'm sure Jim talked to them and explained what happened to Grandpa." Caitlynn flinched and stiffened at the mention of her grandfather, but the hand on her back didn't stop its slow circles. "And they've had a whole week to calm down."

"Marcie will still be angry."

"Perhaps. But if you go in and maybe apologize for your mistake, I'm sure she'll be okay again. Everyone makes mistakes, Caty," Mom reminded her. "The trick is to learn from them and move on, right?"

Caitlynn leaned in to her mother and sighed. "I guess."

"You already told Grandpa you were going back. He'll be waiting to hear all about it when we visit tomorrow."

Caitlynn sighed again but nodded. "Okay. I'll try," she said.

* * *

"Caitlynn's back!" Amanda cried when Caitlynn entered the

changing room. "We didn't think you were going to come back. Where were you?"

"How's your Grandpa?" Meghan asked.

"Are you back to stay now?"

"Yeah, I guess I'm back to stay," Caitlynn answered slowly, bewildered.

"Well, that's good," Meghan said, shoving her clothes in her bag. She tossed it over her shoulder and stood waiting for the others. "'Cause it wasn't much fun when you weren't here."

Amanda patted her shoulder as she passed. "You're just in time, too. We're going to start learning back-flip turns!"

"You guys aren't mad at me?" Caitlynn asked as they walked out to the pool deck together.

"Why would we be mad at you? Oh, because of the relay?" Meghan guessed. She waved her hand at Caitlynn. "Whatever, Caty. I false started *dozens* of times when I was just learning."

"But what about Marcie ..."

"What about her?" Amanda demanded. She tossed her bag on the bleachers and tucked some loose hairs into her bathing cap. "She's always mad at somebody. But Jim explained about your Grandpa." Amanda shrugged. "Marcie's fine."

Caitlynn breathed a sigh of relief. She adjusted her bathing cap, slipped her goggles on, and joined the others. It felt so good to dive into the cold water! She flexed the muscles of her arms and legs slowly as she swam her warm-up lengths. The tension and stress of the last week floated away and her mind felt lighter.

Here she could concentrate on that pesky breaststroke kick, or on not bumping her head when she did backstroke. She could try that bilateral breathing Jim was teaching them or experiment with the hand paddles. She could try not to bump her head when they worked on the back-flip turn. She didn't have to think about Grandpa or wonder when he would come home.

And after all these weeks, she wasn't even thinking about her old soccer team, wondering what the girls were doing and if they'd won any of their games. Her mom had mentioned returning to the team in January, but Caitlynn was surprised to realize she didn't want to give up swimming. Even when she messed up and struggled with the strokes, she still liked coming to the practices.

The only time it wasn't good to be back was when she automatically looked into the bleachers after she'd done something particularly well. There was no Grandpa sitting there watching, his cap in his lap, his coat folded neatly beside him. No Grandpa to give her a thumbs-up or a little wave or even, sometimes, a small frown and a shake of the head when she did something she shouldn't.

"How's your grandfather doing, Caitlynn?" Jim asked halfway through practice. He knelt down at the edge of the pool.

"I saw him this morning," Caitlynn said. She rested her arms on the deck and let her legs float out behind her. "He can't talk very good right now but Mom says that'll get better."

"Well, that's good to know. We used to have some interesting chats while he was waiting for you."

Caitlynn looked surprised. And then she got suspicious. "About me?" she demanded.

Jim laughed. "No, not about you. About swimming. He's given me some good coaching tips."

"He's always coaching me," Caitlynn said, rolling her eyes. "He even coaches my brother about playing ball hockey. Grandpa never even played ball hockey! He's always telling him to take one skill at a time and perfect that, rather than trying to tackle the whole thing. It drives Colin crazy. He tells me the same thing."

"Your Grandpa is a smart man, Caty," Jim said standing. "He knows that the things we learn in one sport can be applied to other ones, too."

Caitlynn made a face and Jim laughed again. "You tell him I said hi, okay? And tell him I'm going to come and visit soon, to get some more coaching advice."

* * *

The next morning Caitlynn, Colin, and their mom went to the hospital to visit Grandpa. He was sitting up in bed and looked happy to see them. Caitlynn let her mom and brother visit for a bit before climbing onto the bed and nestling in close to Grandpa's good right side.

"Ow my Cay-Ba?" he asked, hugging her close.

"I went to practice yesterday," she told him. "Jim says to say hi." Grandpa nodded. "He says to tell you he's going to come and visit."

"I ike im. Guu man."

"I missed you so much yesterday," Caitlynn whispered.

"I mish oo too."

"It's too hard," Caitlynn said. "I don't think I can go by myself. I need you there."

"Oh, Cay-Ba. Oo an oo it. Oo an."

"I don't think I *can* do it, Grandpa!"

Grandpa wiggled a bit and made Caitlynn sit up. He looked hard at her, his pale blue eyes holding her bright blue ones as he struggled with what he wanted to say.

"Oo an me," he said, pointing first at Caitlynn then at himself, "may a pac."

Caitlynn looked to her mother for help, so she came over and stood next to the bed. Grandpa repeated himself and she nodded.

"A pact, an agreement," she translated. Grandpa nodded, looking at Caitlynn.

Caitlynn looked doubtful, but she kept listening.

"I erk ... ard get edder, oo erk ard ... aa ool."

"You work hard to get better, and I work hard at the pool," Caitlynn said, finally figuring it out after a couple of tries.

Grandpa nodded and cupped her cheek with his hand. Caitlynn leaned into the warmth and put her own hand over his wrinkled one. She sighed but nodded.

"Okay, Grandpa," she said. "It's a deal."

"I uf oo, Cay-Ba."

"I love you, too, Grandpa."

11

Bad News

The house felt strange without Grandpa in it. It was almost like when her dad had first left and Caitlynn, Colin, and their mom had wandered around, bumping into each other, not sure what to do with themselves. But gradually things settled back into their old ways. Caitlynn and Colin went to school each morning and their mother went to the hospital. She spent the day with Grandpa and was home when they finished school in the afternoon. Three times each week she took them to visit Grandpa.

Caitlynn kept up her end of their agreement. She tried hard every practice and ignored Marcie as much as she could. And Grandpa kept getting stronger and stronger. Sometimes when they went to visit, he was sitting in a wheelchair by the window and Caitlynn got to push him in the halls for a little while.

As the days and weeks went by, Caitlynn became quite good at understanding her grandfather's speech, although there were still times when no matter how many times he repeated himself she still couldn't figure out what he was saying. Sometimes they laughed until it hurt over Caitlynn's translations.

"I passed a math test today, Grandpa," she told him one afternoon. "It was pretty hard, but I studied."

"Oooh shmaa gul, Cay-Ba," Grandpa told her, patting her arm.

"I'm what?"

"Shmaa gul."

"A small gull?" Caitlynn asked, but Grandpa shook his head.

"Shmaaa gul," he said, speaking more slowly.

"A smile gull? That doesn't make any sense!"

Grandpa smiled his new smile — the one where the left side of his mouth didn't move, just the right. Caitlynn called it his gangster grin. She started giggling. She put her hand to her mouth and tried to choke it back.

"A smelly girl?"

Grandpa made a sound that sounded like a cross between a laugh and a snort. Bits of spit flew from his mouth. Caitlynn started laughing harder, holding her stomach.

"I know!" she said, containing her laughter long enough to speak. "A smart girl. I'm a smart girl!"

Grandpa held up his right hand and Caitlynn gently slapped it. They grinned happily at each other.

"That was a toughie, Grandpa," she told him. "I didn't think I'd ever get it."

* * *

In the middle of January, Mom announced that Grandpa would be able to leave the hospital by the end of the month. Caitlynn hugged herself tightly, pure joy bubbling up inside and threatening to spill out in a happy dance. After all this long, horrible time, Grandpa would finally be coming home. There would be Grandpa at the dinner table eating with them and listening to the talk. He would be sitting in his chair waiting for her when she came home from school each day.

They would go to Silver Valley together every Tuesday. And on Monday, Wednesday, and Friday they would go to the pool for swim practice. Of course, it might take a while for Grandpa to be allowed to drive again, but surely Mrs. Hamada would take Grandpa too? Oh, it was too good to be true! She absolutely couldn't wait.

The very next afternoon Caitlynn opened the door to Grandpa's suite and went down the stairs. She hadn't been down there since before his stroke. It was likely dusty and in need of some cleaning. Caitlynn had decided she would get everything ready as a surprise for Grandpa when he came home. She'd even been saving her allowance to buy some flowers.

She rushed into the room and stopped, her mouth falling open in disbelief. Before her, stacked one on top of the other, was box after box, all neatly labeled: *Books*, *Kitchen*, *Dishes*, *Winter Clothes*. The worn, green sofa and the table were gone. The television set and the bookcase were missing too, and the little table and chairs.

Slowly Caitlynn walked through the small space. Grandpa's life had been packed up and was obviously being moved. Where would he go? Why wouldn't he stay here? This was his home! Caitlynn dashed back up the stairs, taking them two at a time in her haste, tripping at the top and nearly falling.

"MOM!" she cried, running through the house frantically. "MOM! What's happened to Grandpa's stuff? Mom?"

She finally found her, talking on the phone in her bedroom. Mom set the phone down after saying a quick goodbye, and turned to face Caitlynn.

"What have you done with Grandpa's stuff? It's all packed up and his furniture is gone."

"Come sit here, Caitlynn, beside me," her mother said softly, patting the bed. Caitlynn sat, eyeing her mother suspiciously. Her mother took Caitlynn's hands in her own and held them tightly. "I need you to listen carefully, Caitlynn, and let me finish speaking before you say a word. Will you do that for me?"

Slowly, reluctantly, Caitlynn nodded. "The thing is, Grandpa can't live here with us when he leaves the hospital." Before Caitlynn could speak, Mom held up a finger and continued. "We don't have the right house for a wheelchair. And he can't be left alone in case he falls or needs help with things."

Caitlynn's thoughts flew through her brain so quickly she couldn't even fix on one. Grandpa wasn't coming home to live here. That was all she could focus on.

"It would be very expensive to have someone come in and stay all day with him. We can't afford that. So the doctors and I decided that the best place for Grandpa is a nursing home. When Grandpa leaves the hospital next week, he'll be moving to Silver Valley."

* * *

Grandpa was sitting in the chair by the window when Caitlynn arrived for her visit the next day. She gave him a kiss and stood beside him, holding his hand.

"It's pretty cold outside today," she told him, nodding toward the window. "The weatherman said we might get snow. If it snows, I'll build you a snowman, okay? And take a picture of it."

"'Kay," Grandpa agreed.

"Did you stand up today, Grandpa? With your standing frame thing?"

"No shan oo-ay," he told her, his words coming out more garbled than usual. Caitlynn caught his eye and they looked at each other for a long, silent minute. Grandpa's blue eyes weren't as bright and cheerful as they usually were.

"Mom said you can't come home," she said at last. "She says you have to go to Silver Valley."

Grandpa didn't answer. He dropped Caitlynn's hand and turned to look out the window, shaking his head, sadly.

"We have to think of a way to change her mind, all their minds. You and me, we'll think and think, okay?" She grabbed at his hand again and held it tightly. The old, familiar strength wasn't there anymore. Before, if Grandpa had grabbed her by the hand or wrist, there was no way she could have pulled away. Now if she pulled at all, he would just let go.

"Old, Cay-Ba, oosh les," he said so softly that Caitlynn had to lean over to hear him.

12

Silver Valley

Grandpa moved to Silver Valley on Thursday while Caitlynn was in her social studies class. While Mrs. Singh yakked on about the provinces and their capitals, Grandpa was put on a stretcher and wheeled to a special ambulance. While Caitlynn read in her textbook about when each province joined Confederation, Grandpa was driven across town to Silver Valley and wheeled down the long hall to his new room.

While Caitlynn wrote Fredericton by New Brunswick's tiny space on the map, Grandpa was transferred from the stretcher to a wheelchair. They put the chair by the window so he could look outside at the freshly fallen snow in the garden. Caitlynn pressed hard on British Columbia with her yellow pencil crayon and snapped the tip. She reached for the orange pencil and started colouring Alberta.

Mom was probably bustling around Grandpa's new room, straightening knick-knacks, putting out his pictures. She was probably going on and on about how *nice* everything was — the food, the nurses, the other residents. Well everything had been *nice* at home! Her mother was a great cook and Grandpa's suite downstairs was more than just a nasty little room with white walls!

The orange tip snapped. Caitlynn stared down at the word *Calgary* printed in the centre of Alberta. Half of the word was

coloured white and half was orange. Caitlynn banged her fist on her desk.

"What's the matter, Caty?" Jenna asked. They'd been allowed to sit together for this activity, something Caitlynn usually loved. But this morning Caitlynn didn't even care.

"Nothing," she snapped.

"What'd I do?" Jenna wanted to know, leaning across Caitlynn's desk. "Are you mad at me?"

Caitlynn brushed away the sudden tears and shook her head. "No, I'm not mad at you," she mumbled.

"Are you mad because you got the capital wrong for Alberta?" Jenna asked, pointing at Caitlynn's map.

Despite herself, Caitlynn giggled. She shook her head and sniffed. "Grandpa's moving to Silver Valley this morning," she explained.

"Oh. Right."

Caitlynn looked at her friend. Jenna looked concerned, but how could she help? Nothing she could do would change the fact that Grandpa wasn't moving home. Caitlynn sniffed again and Jenna patted her shoulder.

"It'll be okay, Caty," she said. "You'll see. Silver Valley is so close to your house, you'll be able to go all the time."

Caitlynn knew her friend was trying to make her feel better, but it wasn't helping. Mrs. Singh paused at Caitlynn's desk.

"Caitlynn, what is the capital of Alberta?" she asked, tapping the province with a red-tipped finger.

"Edmonton," Caitlynn muttered, staring at the uneven colouring on her map, at the broken pencil tips scattered across the top of her desk. Mrs. Singh tapped the desk once more and then moved away.

Caitlynn picked up her eraser and scrubbed hard at the offending word. The orange smudged with the black pencil and

left a mess. She scrubbed harder and harder until Alberta finally tore. Caitlynn grabbed the paper, crumpled it into a ball, and threw it away. She sat there, breathing heavily, her anger not lessened one little bit.

* * *

On Saturday, Mom took Caitlynn and Colin to Silver Valley to visit. Caitlynn could hardly eat breakfast. Her stomach was tied in knots and she thought she might be sick. She kept glancing at the closed door leading to Grandpa's suite. The brightly coloured *Welcome Home* sign Caitlynn had made was hanging on the door. She got up from the table and tore it down, ripping the paper until it was confetti in her fingers and around her feet on the floor. She picked up all the pieces and put them in the recycling bin.

The front garden at Silver Valley was snow-covered and lonely. The trees were skeletons, their icy branches reaching out sadly, and the shrubs were small, white mounds hunched against the elements. Caitlynn walked more slowly as they approached the doors.

Inside was the same as before — the same heat and smell, the same people in the same spots waiting. She saw Old Joe, his head slumped to one side as he snored, and Mrs. Dawson tied in her chair. Caitlynn looked away quickly from Mrs. Dawson and followed after her mother down the long hall. They stopped in front of a closed door. On the wall was a small folder with a photograph and a card.

"This isn't Grandpa's room," Colin said, pointing to the strange man in the picture. "This says Ivan Pulinsky."

Mom laughed. "I know. They haven't changed that yet, but they will. Grandpa has only been here a couple of days."

"What happened to Old Ivan?"

"I don't know, Colin, to be honest. No one told me," their mother said, smoothing her hair and straightening her sweater.

"Probably he croaked," Colin decided.

"You be quiet, Colin!" Caitlynn cried.

"Colin," their mother warned, shooting him a "keep quiet" glance. She knocked three times on the door and pushed it open, hustling Caitlynn and her brother in ahead of her.

"Hi, Dad!" She leaned over and kissed Grandpa's cheek. "Look who's come to visit."

Caitlynn hung back while Colin said hello. Then she moved slowly up beside Grandpa's wheelchair. They looked at each other. Grandpa's face was gray and tired-looking in the dim light of the room.

"Hey, Grandpa," she said softly.

"Lo, Cay-Ba."

"Dad, why don't you have any lights on in here? It's so dark!" While Mom bustled around the room, Colin perched on the edge of the bed and was very intent on his fingernails.

"How was breakfast?" Caitlynn asked at last, struggling to think of something to talk about. It wasn't usually this difficult to talk to Grandpa. She had to ask again before she understood his answer: Not as good as her mother's.

"Mom made waffles this morning. Would you like me to bring you one next time?" Caitlynn offered. "I could sneak it in for you."

"S'okay. Ow ool?" he asked, taking in both children with his eyes.

"I did good on a test this week in spelling. I got only two wrong," Caitlynn told him.

He nodded at her then turned to Colin. Colin looked blankly at his sister. "What'd he say?" he asked.

"How's school," Caitlynn snapped. If Colin had *tried* to talk to Grandpa in the hospital, he'd understand. But all he had ever done on their visits was answer the questions their mother translated.

As Colin told Grandpa about a science-fair project he was working on, Caitlynn looked around at Grandpa's room. Her mother was fussing with some things on the nightstand. There was a clock — the old-fashioned kind that ticked — and a glass dish that had always been filled with candy but was empty now. There were framed pictures of Caitlynn, Colin, and their mother, even one of Maggie. Little knick-knacks sat on the dresser and the bedside table, and there were flowers in a vase near the window.

The pretty patchwork quilt Grandma had made years ago, the one that always lived on the green couch, was spread across the bottom of the bed. But it didn't feel like a home. It felt like a hospital, a hospital you didn't leave.

Caitlynn was very glad when her mother decided they'd stayed long enough and it was time to go home. She hurriedly kissed Grandpa goodbye before running from the room and out of the building. She didn't wait for her family, but kept going down the hill. Her lungs burned and her legs ached, but she ran all the way home. She had to stand on the front steps shivering until her mom and brother caught up.

In her mind, Caitlynn saw Grandpa, tied in his wheelchair, staring out the window. He looked so old and miserable! How could her mother leave him in that awful place? He didn't like the food; all he had was a tiny little room, and there were all those old people who just sat there, day after day. Who would he have good yaks with? Or play games with? Was he just going to sit and wait like everyone else?

"Probably he croaked," Colin had said about that Ivan guy.

Caitlynn shuddered, but what else would have happened to him? Maybe he went to live somewhere else. No, probably he had died, leaving his bed available for some other old person. Now Grandpa could use that bed until he, too, died. Great, salty tears swelled in Caitlynn's eyes. Someday would some other man get Grandpa's bed once he had died? A moan escaped her and the tears ran down her cheeks.

A few minutes later her mother and Colin came up the walk. Colin opened the door and flew inside, thundering up the stairs. Mom stopped on the step beside Caitlynn and rested her hand on Caitlynn's shoulder.

"Let's go in the house, Sweetie," she said. "It's too cold out here."

She guided Caitlynn inside, and they sat in the living room. The space right in front of the window, where Grandpa's old black recliner used to sit, was empty. The recliner had been sold along with most of Grandpa's other furniture. There was nowhere to put it in his room at Silver Valley. Fresh tears filled Caitlynn's eyes.

"I know the first time is rough," Mom said, gently rubbing Caitlynn's back. "But Grandpa will get used to his new place and you'll get used to seeing him there, and soon it won't seem so strange anymore."

"You sent him there to die," Caitlynn accused, raising her head to glare at her mother. "I know that old Ivan Pul-whatever died. I know Colin was right. He died and now Grandpa gets his bed until he dies. How could you do that? He doesn't want to be there waiting to die. He wants to be home."

"Oh, Caitlynn," her mother said with a great, weary sigh. "I know this is so hard for you. But Sweetie, what else could I do? I've explained why he can't live here. And there is no reason why Grandpa can't live a long, long time still. Silver Valley is a very nice place. No, it isn't home, but it will become more homelike as Grandpa gets used to it. And once he is better able to move around on his own, he'll come here as often as possible."

She sighed again. "It's not a very nice part of getting elderly and getting sick. But Grandpa has talked with you about this before. And he really needs you to support him now."

Maggie jumped up on the couch. Caitlynn put an arm around the dog's neck and buried her face in the warm, soft fur. "What about Maggie?" she asked, her voice muffled.

"What about her?"

"You always said you didn't have time for a dog. You're not going to send Maggie away like you did Grandpa, are you?" Caitlynn demanded, raising her head to look at her mother.

Her mother flinched and blinked. She looked away before she spoke. "No, Maggie isn't going anywhere. You and Colin have been doing a very good job of helping to care for her, and we'll all have to keep that up. Maggie can visit Grandpa at Silver Valley as often as she likes."

Caitlynn leaned against her mother's arm. "He looked so unhappy, Mom," she said. "It made me feel bad."

"I know, Caitlynn." She stroked Caitlynn's curls. "It makes me feel sad too. But the best way we can help Grandpa get used to his new home is to be positive and cheerful. We'll get him some nice plants and you can do some of your great artwork. You'll see, it won't take long for Grandpa to be his old self again."

13

Focus

The Friday before Valentine's Day, Jim announced another swim meet at the end of the month.

"I'd like to enter you this time, Caty," he said when the others had started jumping in the pool.

Caitlynn fidgeted with her goggles, her big toe poking at a crack in the tiled floor. She stubbornly refused to look at Jim.

"You haven't been in a meet since November," her coach continued after a few seconds. "I know the last one wasn't the greatest experience for you, but it's important to try again ..."

Caitlynn felt a hot wave of anger start to build. He didn't understand anything! Grandpa's stroke, Marcie's angry, accusing face — it was all too fresh, too painful. Caitlynn continued to say nothing.

Finally Jim sighed. "Well, maybe next time then, hmm? You go ahead and get in."

Relieved to be let off the hook, Caitlynn dove in and swam her warm-up lengths. By the time she'd finished, Aiden, Amanda, and Meghan were waiting for her at the wall.

"Hey, guess what," Aiden said. "Jim says I can try doing butterfly at the next meet!"

"Yeah? That's nice. I've been practising my kick, wanna see?" Caitlynn asked.

She grabbed a board from the deck. Holding her feet and knees tightly together, she dolphin-kicked down the lane a short way and then turned around and came back.

Aiden looked impressed. "That's pretty good," he agreed. "But can you do it with your arms at the same time?"

Caitlynn stuck her tongue out at him. "Just 'cause you're so great at it," she muttered and Aiden laughed.

"What's so funny?" Amanda asked.

"Nothing," Caitlynn said at the same time Aiden said, "Caitlynn can dolphin-kick."

"That's great, Caty," Amanda said with a grin. "But can you do the arms too?"

"Oh, be quiet, both of you!" Caitlynn cried, splashing them both until Jim's whistle blew.

Caitlynn had been working hard on her butterfly stroke. Aiden did it really well, and so did Marcie, although she had been disqualified in the last swim meet for touching the wall with only one hand. Even Caitlynn knew you had to use two hands!

They practised for a long time. Jim had a whole bunch of new drills to try, but Caitlynn's favourite was the one in which they pretended to be mermaids. She kept her knees and feet tightly together, pushed off from the wall and, doing her dolphin kick, swam along the bottom of the pool, her arms tight at her sides. When she ran out of breath, she popped to the surface, and then did it again, all the way to the other side of the pool. Sometimes she rolled over on her back.

"That looked good, guys," Jim called out. "Let's try with the arms this time. Left arm by itself, right arm by itself, then two strokes of both arms together." He showed them what he meant and sent them off.

This was the hard part. Caitlynn struggled to get both arms

over at the same time — and she had to remember to keep her head tucked and to keep her feet and knees together and to kick at the right time. Her brain felt like it might explode as she tried to keep track of everything. Somehow she managed to get to the other end.

"Your arms are supposed to go over *together*," Marcie said from the other lane.

"Your hands are supposed to touch the wall *together* too," Caitlynn retorted. "But they don't always, do they?"

Marcie's face turned bright red, but she said nothing as Jim approached. He gave them all some more instructions and then everyone pushed off again. Just before Caitlynn took her turn, Jim stopped her.

"You are trying really hard, Caty," he said, crouching down. "But you're trying to tackle too many things at once. Remember our conversation about focusing on one skill at a time?" Caitlynn nodded. "Well, for now, I'd like you to do that. You are doing a good job with your kick. So let's forget about it now and focus on getting those arms over together. That's the only thing I want you to worry about, okay?"

Caitlynn nodded again hesitantly. Forget everything else? She looked down the length of the pool at the others and longed to do it perfectly like Aiden or Marcie. She took a deep breath and pushed off the wall. Left arm, right arm, stroke, stroke. She forgot about her legs, forgot about keeping her chin tucked. All she thought of was getting her arms over at the same time. Left arm, right arm, stroke, stroke. Arms, arms, arms. And then, suddenly, she did it! And she did it again!

She finished her two lengths and stood up, grinning. "I did it! Did you see? I did it!" she cried. "They went over together!"

"You did it, Caitlynn," Jim said. "That was great."

Caitlynn couldn't stop grinning. Aiden gave her a high five

and Amanda and Meghan clapped her on the shoulder. Then she turned and overheard Marcie say to the girl standing next to her, "Oh, brother."

Some of the joy went out of Caitlynn. Sharp retorts rose up inside and were almost out of her mouth when she remembered her agreement with Grandpa. She had to try her best at practice and she had to try to ignore Marcie. She closed her mouth tightly and grabbed a kickboard from the pile. Her anger gradually subsided as she kicked as hard as she could through the water.

* * *

"Happy Valentine's Day, Grandpa!" Caitlynn shouted. She came running through the door carrying a big balloon, a container of sugar cookies, a hand-made card, and a big box of Grandpa's favourite chocolate-covered gingers.

As usual, Grandpa was sitting by the window, a blanket over his legs, his old gray cardigan over his shoulders. The snowman Caitlynn had made out in the garden grinned crookedly at them and waved its stick arms.

"Look what I brought you!" she said, piling everything in Grandpa's lap. "The cookies are from me and Mom, and the chocolates are from me. The balloon is from Colin. And look, I made the card! Isn't it neat? Look how you open it and there's a picture!"

"S-booiful, Cay-Ba," Grandpa told her. He made the balloon bob on the end of its string. He touched the box of chocolates and the tin holding the cookies.

"Would you like to try a cookie? They're awesome. We tried a new recipe and Mom even let me buy sugar crystals this time!"

Caitlynn opened the tin and held it out to her grandfather,

but he shook his head. "No, sank you, Cay-Ba," he said. "No ungee jus no."

A little of the bounce went out of Caitlynn, but she shrugged and replaced the lid, then put the cookie tin on the table. She stood silently for several minutes while Grandpa stared out the window or at his hands. Since he'd moved to Silver Valley two weeks before, this was what had happened every time Caitlynn visited. How long was this adjusting supposed to take?

"Did you do some standing this week? Was Sally in to work on your speech with you?" she asked.

"Oh, no shtanin' thish week," Grandpa said without turning from the window. "No talkin'."

"Why not?" Caitlynn asked, shaking his shoulder gently. "You're supposed to keep working at getting better, remember? I didn't fight with Marcie yesterday, even though she said mean things. And I can almost do the butterfly! I'm working *hard* at the pool!"

"A goo, Cay-Ba," Grandpa told her with a small smile. "bu-a-fly."

"But what about you?"

Grandpa sighed and touched Caitlynn's hair. "I'm too ole, Cay-Ba."

"But remember? You told me to do one thing at a time. And it worked! I just focused on my arms going over my head together and I did it!" Caitlynn cried eagerly, grabbing Grandpa's hand and squeezing it. "So maybe that's what you need to do too. Just practise one thing!"

Grandpa pulled his hand away and it fell back into his lap. "Wha's the use?" he asked softly, more to himself than to Caitlynn.

"But Mom says if you keep working with the therapists, you'll keep getting stronger and your talking will get clearer,"

Caitlynn tried again. "Don't you want that? Don't you want to walk again?"

Grandpa turned away from the window and looked sadly at Caitlynn. He patted her hand, but he didn't answer her.

14

Grandpa Gives Up

Grandpa? You awake?" Caitlynn called softly into the dimly lit room. She flicked on the lights as she came in.

Grandpa adjusted his position in the wheelchair and squinted in the sudden brightness.

"I need your help! I have this project for school — on polar bears — and I can't do it myself. Mom tried to help but she's not as good as you at finding stuff. I brought all my books and papers," Caitlynn said, spilling everything out onto the bed. She picked up a *National Geographic* with a large polar bear on the cover and turned to look at her grandfather. He looked surprised, and then shook his head.

"But you *always* help me with my projects. I brought a whole mess of books. It would be great if we could go on the Internet — don't they have computers here? I thought I saw a computer room. Maybe we could go there next. Here," Caitlynn said, pausing to hand Grandpa the *National Geographic*, "you look through this one and let me know if you find anything. I'll look through these."

But Grandpa didn't open the magazine. He frowned at Caitlynn and handed it back to her with a shake of his head. "Ash Mom, Cay-Ba."

Disappointment filled Caitlynn and she blinked back tears.

"But you always help me with this stuff. You're really good at it ..." Her voice trailed off as Grandpa shook his head again, then turned to look out the window.

Slowly Caitlynn gathered her materials and shoved them in her backpack. She slipped the straps over her shoulders and left the room, trying hard not to cry.

That night Caitlynn knocked on Colin's bedroom door.

"What do you want, Brat?" he asked.

"I was wondering if you could help me with this project I have for school," she began. "It's due in a couple of days. I've been trying by myself but ..."

"What's it on?" Colin asked.

"Polar bears. I have some stuff. Grandpa usually helps me, but he wouldn't. And Mom is busy." Caitlynn held out her notes hopefully. The fact that he hadn't slammed the door in her face yet was definitely a good sign.

"Oh yeah? Did you check the Internet?" he asked, flipping through what she already had.

"There's too much stuff. I don't know what to look for. When I did a search for polar bears I got 879,000 sites!"

Colin laughed and nodded. "You have to be more specific than that. Come on, I'll help you for a bit."

A half hour later, Colin sat back in his chair and crossed his arms. "Have you got enough now?" he asked.

"Yeah, thanks," Caitlynn said. She had pages of notes now, and they'd even made a recording. Even Grandpa wouldn't have been able to do that. "Colin?"

"What?" he asked, closing down the computer.

"Why is Grandpa taking so long to adjust to living at Silver Valley? Why won't he try to get better?"

"He's pissed off that he couldn't come home," Colin told her with a shrug. "I would be too."

"Yeah, but he's always telling us to make the best of things and to try our hardest. He won't try to walk, he's just giving up."

Colin stopped playing with the mouse and turned to look at Caitlynn. "I don't know, Caitlynn."

"Do you miss him?" she asked softly.

For a long time Colin said nothing, just looked at the blank computer screen. Caitlynn was about to ask her question again when he spoke. "Yeah. I miss him, even his nagging," he said. "Nothing's the same without him here."

Caitlynn looked down at the pile of notes in her lap. "No, nothing's the same," she agreed.

* * *

"I'm here, Grandpa!" Caitlynn called as she and Maggie entered the room. "And I brought someone else this time!"

She let go of Maggie's leash and the little dog ran to Grandpa. She put her front paws on his leg, her tail wagging furiously. Grandpa rubbed her ears and scratched under her chin, and Maggie made little noises deep in her throat. Caitlynn perched on the bed and watched, smiling.

It had been hard, coming back to visit again and again, only to find Grandpa quiet and withdrawn. But Caitlynn refused to give up on him. She came several times a week, sometimes with Maggie, sometimes alone. She talked even when he wouldn't and she always tried to bring some little treat with her.

"I knew this would cheer you up." she said. "Maggie pulled me all the way up the hill! I thought she'd pull my arms off, Grandpa. I'm sorry I didn't make it in to visit this week. I had a bad cold and Mom said I couldn't come. We didn't want you to get sick. I'm better now. Hey, guess what? We're reading a new book at school …"

"Where'sh Maggie?" Grandpa interrupted, shifting in his chair.

Caitlynn found Maggie sniffing at Grandpa's shoes. She gave her a pat and returned to the bed. "She's fine, Grandpa. Just sniffing. Maggie's a good girl. She won't get into anything." She nibbled on the rough edge of a fingernail and swung her legs, banging them against the metal edge.

"Shtop at Cay-lyn."

Caitlynn blushed, confused, but she stopped. Suddenly she jumped up. "Let's take Maggie out and say hi to some of the others, okay? Old Joe saw us come in — he'll want a visit." She picked up Maggie's leash and held it out to Grandpa. "You take Maggie and I'll push your chair."

But Grandpa didn't take the leash. "Oo go, Cay-Ba. I'm ired."

"You're always tired!" Caitlynn flung the leash away and it struck Maggie on the back. The little dog cowered, her tail wagging uncertainly.

"Ont it er!" Grandpa snapped.

"I didn't mean to! Why won't you do anything?" she cried, tears springing to her eyes. "All you do is sit in this dark little room. You aren't trying to adjust or anything!"

"Oo ont unershtan," Grandpa said slowly, turning away from her to look out the window. "Not shay as I wush."

"You're right, you aren't the same," Caitlynn agreed. "My old Grandpa *never* gave up. He always told me I had to keep trying when things were hard and focus on one small thing at a time until I got it."

Grandpa didn't answer. Caitlynn balled her fingers into fists and hit the bed as hard as she could. It didn't help ease the anger inside. "You also told me that even if your outsides changed, your insides wouldn't — but you *lied*."

She grabbed Maggie's leash and stormed to the door. She

paused there and turned around to face him again. He was looking at her sadly, but did nothing to bring her back. "I'm never
coming back here again," she cried. *"Never!"*

15

Falling Apart

Caitlynn slept poorly that night and woke up in a foul, dark mood. She glared at her brother as she ate breakfast. "Move your stupid elbows!" she snapped, shoving at Colin's bony arms, trying to make space for the comics and her bowl.

"Bug off, Brat!" Colin shoved back, a littler harder.

"Stop hogging the whole table!"

One good shove and two cereal bowls and their contents were lying in a dripping mess on the floor. Caitlynn could feel her mother's disappointed glare all the way from where she stood at the counter.

"I had a long day yesterday and a lousy sleep," Mom said in a tightly controlled voice, "so I'm liable to say something I'll regret if I comment on what just happened. I'm going upstairs to dress. When I come down again, that mess had better be wiped up and both of you had better be ready to go to school."

Colin leveled an evil stare at Caitlynn as Mom left the room, but Caitlynn was suddenly tired of the battle. She got a dishcloth and wiped carefully at the spilled milk, wringing the cloth out several times before she was done. Colin picked up the bowls and spoons, rinsed them, filled them again, and set them on the table. Neither of them spoke as they ate.

The day didn't get any better.

"Hey, Caitlynn," Jenna called, running to join her on the playground. "Did you remember to bring back that book I loaned you?"

"What book?" Caitlynn asked, spinning idly on the tire swing, not looking at Jenna. She knew the book, she just couldn't find it. She'd looked everywhere and it had disappeared.

Jenna scowled. "*The Secret Garden*. You begged me for it for days. I want to lend it to my cousin and she's coming over this weekend. You promised to return it by the end of this week."

"Oh, that one," Caitlynn said. "I don't know where it is."

"What do you mean you don't know where it is?"

"I'll find it, Jenna. Chill out! I just don't know where it is right this minute. Jeez!" Caitlynn spun herself harder until her curls whipped out around her head. Suddenly the swing jerked to a stop and Jenna was glaring at her, her hands gripping the chains.

"I *want* my book back, Caitlynn Sinclair!"

"I'll give it back to you, Jenna!"

"You said you'd bring it back today and you didn't. You *lied*."

Caitlynn jumped up from the swing and confronted her friend. "I'm sorry I can't give it to you RIGHT THIS SECOND," she screamed. "Take a pill! I'll find it."

"You've lost my favourite book, Caitlynn. I'll never forgive you! Never!"

Before Caitlynn could answer Jenna had run off.

* * *

That afternoon at the pool, Jim announced a new game. He had them all swim down to the shallow end.

"All right, here's what we're going to do," Jim said when

they were all arranged with lots of space between them. "Starting in a standing position, hands in the air, wait for my whistle. When you hear the whistle, you're going to do a somersault in the water, stand up again, and finish with your hands in the air. The last one standing each time will be eliminated. The swimmer who makes it to the very end without being eliminated will be the winner."

Caitlynn and Amanda exchanged bewildered glances. Caitlynn thought of the mess she made of somersaults at the wall — and even on dry land — and groaned. She'd be the first to go!

When the whistle blew Caitlynn pushed off the bottom of the pool as hard as she could and dove forward, tucking her knees to her chest. Using her arms, she struggled to get her legs around and back to the tiled bottom of the pool. Finally, sputtering, she raised her arms in the air and opened her eyes to look around. She wasn't last!

"Good job, guys! That was a really good effort," Jim called from the deck. "But I think Amanda was last this time. Sorry Amanda."

Amanda shrugged and walked to the edge of the pool. Caitlynn breathed a sigh of relief and got ready to go again. Slowly the number of kids in the pool got smaller and smaller, but still Caitlynn managed to hang on.

Finally there were only three swimmers left: Caitlynn, Marcie, and Aiden. They spread out again and put their arms in the air, ready to go. She heard the whistle and flipped over, got to her feet, and looked around. She was first!

"You cheated, Caitlynn Sinclair," Marcie cried as she came up out of the water last. "Jim! Caitlynn cheated!"

"I did not cheat!" Caitlynn was stung by the accusation. She was no cheater!

"You did! You went in before the whistle, I *saw* you."

"I heard the whistle! You're a liar, Marcie!"

"It wasn't Jim's whistle, it was from the diving pool. You cheated!"

"Girls, that's enough. We'll go again and not count that round. Caitlynn, be sure you hear my whistle. And Marcie, pay attention to what you're doing and don't worry so much about others," Jim said.

Caitlynn's heart was pounding and her shoulders were tight with anger. How dare Marcie accuse her of cheating! The whistle blew and Caitlynn went over, but she wasn't concentrating and her feet got twisted. By the time she came up Marcie and Aiden were standing. She glared at Marcie as she made her way to the side.

Caitlynn grabbed her bag from the bleachers at the end of practice a few minutes later and headed into the girls' change room. After a quick rinse, she found a spot on a bench and began towelling off.

"That was fun, wasn't it?" Meghan asked as she peeled out of her wet swimsuit. "Except I got a nose full of water one time. I hate that."

"It was a stupid game," Caitlynn said, rummaging through her bag for her underwear. "I hope we never play it again."

"You're just sore because you got caught *cheating*," Marcie said from across the room.

Red-hot anger surged through Caitlynn and she spun around, her hand already clenched into a fist. "I am NOT a cheater! You take that back! You only said that 'cause you *lost!*"

"Oh, whatever, Caitlynn. I know you cheated."

She didn't remember consciously deciding to leap across the benches at Marcie, but all of a sudden she was right in front of the other girl, being held back by Meghan and two others as she screamed.

"I'm not a cheater! I don't cheat! You take it back!" Caitlynn cried, her fury growing and growing as she tried to get her hands on Marcie, on anything — hair, skin, clothes. Then suddenly the anger was gone and all that was left was an empty space inside. She sat down on a bench, put her face in her hands, and sobbed.

16

One Step at a Time

Caitlynn was suspended from practice for a week and had to write a letter of apology to Marcie. She didn't mind the suspension, but the letter was another thing.

"What about Marcie? Huh?" she demanded of her mother. "What does *she* have to do?"

"Marcie didn't attack anyone, or try to," Mom explained. "You did."

"Marcie called me —"

"Yes, I know, Caty," her mother agreed. "And it wasn't nice of her. But you *must* control your anger. There is no excuse for blowing up like that."

Hot, angry tears filled Caitlynn's eyes and she balled the piece of paper in her hand. There were lots of excuses for blowing up! The whole long, awful day had been an excuse and the miserable visit to Silver Valley the day before.

"Oh, Caitlynn, Sweetie, I know how much you're hurting. But there are some things you just can't do." Mom kissed Caitlynn's forehead. "I'm working with Grandpa's doctors to help him over this rough time, and I really need you to help by keeping control of your temper. Okay?"

"It's not fair," Caitlynn persisted stubbornly. "None of it."

"No. It's not. Will you promise me to keep to your agreement with Grandpa and work hard at swimming?" her mother asked, rising.

"Grandpa isn't keeping his part ..."

"No. But that doesn't mean you can't keep to yours, right?"

Caitlynn didn't answer. She stabbed her pencil into the pad of paper on her desk.

"Get the letter written, take the week to cool off, and we'll start fresh next week, okay?"

Caitlynn looked up at her mother and sniffed. Finally she nodded. Mom smiled and left the room.

* * *

Returning to swim practice a week later was the hardest thing Caitlynn had ever done. She could feel the eyes of her teammates following her as she approached Marcie, but she took a breath, let it out slowly, and kept going. She'd promised her mother and she'd promised Grandpa, and she was determined to keep her promises.

"What do you want?" Marcie snapped when Caitlynn got near.

"I wanted to give you this letter and to say I'm sorry for trying to attack you. I'm not a cheater, but I shouldn't have tried to hurt you. I'm sorry."

She didn't wait for an answer, but turned and walked away as quickly as she could without running. She hid in the change room, shaking, but relieved it was over, until she heard Jim's whistle.

Once she returned to practice, Caitlynn worked harder than she'd ever worked before. She focused on one thing at a time until she finally mastered the back flip. She did length after length after length of butterfly drills until she could do her arms and legs together. It wasn't the prettiest butterfly stroke in the

world, but Caitlynn was awfully proud of herself when she did
it. She looked up into the bleachers automatically, but of course
there was no Grandpa sitting there watching.

She took several deep breaths and closed her eyes as she
turned away. There was a horrible ache deep inside her. Lots of
times she could ignore it, but sometimes it ached harder and
wouldn't be ignored.

It ached when she watched her mother leave to visit
Grandpa. It ached when something good happened and she
wanted to tell him, but remembered with a jolt that she could
not. It ached when Marcie taunted and Caitlynn had to hold to
her promise and ignore her.

"I'm very proud of the way you've been working so hard,
Caty," Jim told her late in March. "I was hoping I might con-
vince you to enter the next swim meet."

There had been no further mention of swim meets since
Valentine's Day. Caitlynn studied her coach for several minutes
before she finally nodded slowly. "Okay, I'll try," she said.

"That's good, Caty. I think I can put you down for two
lengths of butterfly this time. What do you think?" Jim asked.

Caitlynn's eyes widened and she grinned. "Really? You
think I can do it that good now?"

"Absolutely. I think you're ready to try four lengths of front
crawl again, too," he added with a twinkle in his eye.

Caitlynn laughed and pretended to be sinking. But then Jim
walked away and doubt filled her. Could she do it? Did she
want to, if Grandpa wasn't there to watch? Finally she realized
that she did want to.

* * *

The day of the meet, Caitlynn went with Mrs. Hamada and

Aiden to the pool. Her mother promised to come to watch some of the races, and especially the butterfly, which would be near the end.

It was noisy and crowded at the pool. Seven clubs were entered, and there was no room in the bleachers for all the swimmers, so Caitlynn, Aiden, and the rest of the Clippers found space on the tiled floor to set out their towels and bags.

She was excited about this meet. She was no longer Creepy-Crawly Caitlynn or Slow Sinclair. She could swim all four strokes and had the relay thing figured out. She was going to try 100 metres of front crawl this time, and wouldn't need Jim to pull her out halfway through. Caitlynn even let herself dream of a ribbon. Not first, or even second — but maybe a third?

Wouldn't Grandpa be proud! Except that she wasn't telling him stuff. Caitlynn sighed and picked at her towel. The little ache deep inside never went completely away, and just then it hurt more than usual.

Her first race was two lengths of front crawl, a nice easy one to get started. Caitlynn took her time card and handed it to the timers at the end of her lane, then dropped her towel in the basket behind their chairs. She stretched her shoulders and arms the way Jim had shown them, and moved her neck from side to side, looking around casually as she did. She wasn't expecting her mother until later on.

And yet, Caitlynn thought, wasn't that her mother there by the bleachers? She was standing beside a man in a wheelchair. Caitlynn's throat grew thick and her eyes stung behind her goggles as Grandpa waved at her. Her mother smiled and nodded, encouraging her.

"Swimmers, take your marks!" the starter called, and Caitlynn took her position.

At the gun, she dove from the block as though she could

suddenly fly. She hardly felt the cold water or the burn in her muscles as she sprinted down the pool. *Grandpa was there watching her!* She touched the wall the first time and hurried back the way she had just come. *He'd left his dark little room to come and cheer for her.*

Finally she touched the wall, slapping it with her hand so hard her palm stung. Cheers and screams went up all around her, but she hardly noticed as she pulled herself from the water and ran to where her mother and Grandpa were waiting. She threw her arms around his neck and held on as tightly as she could.

"Goo gul, Cay-Ba," Grandpa said softly, cupping her wet cheek with his hand.

Caitlynn tilted her head back to look up at him, and they smiled at each other.

* * *

Caitlynn held tightly to Maggie's leash with one hand while she pulled open the door of Silver Valley with the other. Maggie bounced excitedly at the end of the leash, twisting herself and Caitlynn into a confused tangle. Laughing, Caitlynn unwrapped them both and they made their way inside.

Grandpa was waiting right inside the door, sitting confidently in his wheelchair. He looked so handsome and strong — not like when he had first moved to Silver Valley three months before. She grinned at him.

"Lo 'Aggie," he said, bending over carefully to pet the dog. "Lo, Cay-Ba."

Caitlynn had become so used to Grandpa's new way of talking she hardly noticed any more. Only once in a while did she have to guess at what he was trying to say to her.

"Ready?" Caitlynn asked, kissing his cheek.

"Eddy."

Caitlynn adjusted Maggie's bandana and nametag, and her own. She attached Grandpa's to his shirt pocket and handed him Maggie's leash. Then, with Caitlynn pushing the wheelchair, they moved slowly forward.

"Hello," she said, approaching Old Joe, "Would you like to visit with Maggie today?" she asked.

"Well, okay," Old Joe said, scratching Maggie's silky ears. "And what kind of dog is she? How old is she?"

"She's a Sheltie and she's five," Caitlynn answered. Grandpa reached over and squeezed her hand tightly while they stood there, together, visiting.

Other books you'll enjoy in the Sports Stories series

Gymnastics
❑ *The Perfect Gymnast* by Michele Martin Bossley #9
Abby's new friend has all the confidence she needs, but she also has a serious problem that nobody but Abby seems to know about.

Riding
❑ *A Way with Horses* by Peter McPhee #11
A young Alberta rider, invited to study show jumping at a posh local riding school, uncovers a secret.

❑ *Riding Scared* by Marion Crook #15
A reluctant new rider struggles to overcome her fear of horses.

❑ *Katie's Midnight Ride* by C. A. Forsyth #16
An ambitious barrel racer finds herself without a horse weeks before her biggest rodeo.

❑ *Glory Ride* by Tamara L. Williams #21
Chloe Anderson fights memories of a tragic fall for a place on the Ontario Young Riders Team.

❑ *Cutting It Close* by Marion Crook #24
In this novel about barrel racing, a young rider finds her horse is in trouble just as she's about to compete in an important event.

❑ *Shadow Ride* by Tamara L. Williams #37
Bronwen has to choose between competing aggressively for herself or helping out a teammate.

Soccer
❑ *Lizzie's Soccer Showdown* by John Danakas #3
When Lizzie asks why the boys and girls can't play together, she finds herself the new captain of the soccer team.

❑ *Alecia's Challenge* by Sandra Diersch #32
Thirteen-year-old Alecia has to cope with a new school, a new step-father,

and friends who have suddenly discovered the opposite sex.

❑ *Offside!* by Sandra Diersch #43
Alecia has to confront a new girl who drives her teammates crazy.

❑ *Heads Up!* by Dawn Hunter and Karen Hunter #45
Do the Warriors really need a new, hot-shot player who skips practice?

❑ *Off the Wall* by Camilla Reghelini Rivers #52
Lizzie loves indoor soccer, and she's thrilled when her little sister gets into the sport. But when their teams are pitted against each other, Lizzie can only warn her sister to watch out.

❑ *Trapped!* by Michele Martin Bossley #53
There's a thief on Jane's soccer team, and everyone thinks it's her best friend, Ashley. Jane must find the true culprit to save both Ashley and the team's morale.

❑ *Soccer Star!* by Jacqueline Guest #61
Samantha longs to show up Carly, the school's reigning soccer star, but her new interest in theatre is taking up a lot of her time. Can she really do it all?

❑ *Miss Little's Losers* by Robert Rayner #64
The Brunswick Valley School soccer team haven't won a game all season long. When their coach resigns, the only person who will coach them is Miss Little … their former kindergarten teacher!

❑ *Just for Kicks* by Robert Rayner #69
When their parents begin taking their games too seriously, it's up to the soccer-mad gang from Brunswick Valley School to reclaim the spirit of their sport.

❑ *Play On* by Sandra Diersch #73
Alecia's soccer team is preparing for the championship game but their game is suffering as the players get distracted by other interests. Can they renew their commitment to their sport in order to make it to the finals?

❑ *Suspended* by Robert Rayner #75
The Brunswick Valley soccer form their own unofficial team after falling

foul to the Principal's Code of Conduct. But will they be allowed to play in the championship game before they get discovered?

❏ *Foul Play* by Beverly Scudamore #79
Remy and Alison play on rival soccer teams. When Remy finds out Alison has a special plan to beat Remy's team in the tournament, she becomes convinced that Alison will sabotage her team's players.

Swimming

❏ *Breathing Not Required* by Michele Martin Bossley #4
Gracie works so hard to be chosen for the solo at synchronized swimming that she almost loses her best friend in the process.

❏ *Water Fight!* by Michele Martin Bossley #14
Josie's perfect sister is driving her crazy, but when she takes up swimming — Josie's sport — it's too much to take.

❏ *Taking a Dive* by Michele Martin Bossley #19
Josie holds the provincial record for the butterfly, but in this sequel to Water Fight! she can't seem to match her own time and might not go on to the nationals.

❏ *Great Lengths* by Sandra Diersch #26
Fourteen-year-old Jessie decides to find out whether the rumours about a new swimmer at her Vancouver club are true.

❏ *Pool Princess* by Michele Martin Bossley #47
In this sequel to *Breathing Not Required*, Gracie must deal with a bully on the new synchro team in Calgary.

❏ *Flip Turn* by Monique Polak #67
When the family situation takes a grim turn, swimmer Victoria finds help — in and out of the pool — from the person she least expects.

❏ *False Start* by Sandra Diersch #78
Caitlynn makes a deal with her grandfather to join a swim team if he'll stay and watch all of her practices. But after Grandpa has a stroke, Caitlynn doesn't want to keep up her end of the deal.